# Enigma of the Carousel Project

RB Parkline

Published by RB Parkline, 2024.

ENIGMA OF THE CAROUSEL PROJECT

**First edition. February 15, 2024.**

Copyright © 2024 RB Parkline.

ISBN: 979-8224204335

Written by RB Parkline.

# Chapter I

Hal wiped the sweat from his forehead, he was tired working in a basement that was hot and dusty. He shook his head disgusted seeing none of the other students were anywhere to be seen. They had all left early. Being an undergraduate at Northwestern University Hal along with four others were assigned to clean the basement that appeared no one had been in for years. The Science department was needing to expand so the University allowed the basement which was underutilized to be converted to a lab. There had been four other undergraduates assigned to the basement but they had all skipped out of the job leaving Hal to finish the work. Since the University was on its summer break Hal had stayed to work which helped pay for his higher education.

Hal stood up walking to old metal bookshelves covered in dust from years of neglect standing against the west wall. He had removed the other bookshelves taking them apart placing the small nuts and bolts in a bag. He knew they would be needed when he put the metal shelves together again. Someone in the University would no doubt need them and he would be putting them together in another room.

The small handheld machine quickly removed the small nuts from the bolts. Hal removed the old shelves, stacking them with the others. He hesitated as he removed the last shelf seeing an old handle on the side of the wall. He looked carefully, seeing the distinctive outline of a door. It appeared to have been painted over several times. He smiled seeing the handle was the same color. He wondered why not just remove the handle instead of painting over it? No doubt some lazy undergraduate was told to paint the room and they chose not to remove the handle painting over it.

When the last of the shelves were stacked neatly against a wall. Hal, who was curious, walked to the strange handle sticking out near the north west corner. He pulled the handle down with effort. Pulling on the handle the door creaked loudly as if in protest, then popped open. Hal looked inside seeing shelves lining the small closet. He flipped the old switch and was surprised the light came on. The shelves were filled with dusty old boxes.

Sighing loudly Hal began taking the boxes out of the closet. Most of the boxes were filed with old books and papers. Some of the boxes had old light covers no longer in style. They were older but looked as if they would still work. Many boxes had what looked like instructor attendance logs. Five boxes on the top shelves were too high for Hal to reach.

He was able to find a small ladder so he climbed up the ladder reaching above his head grasping an old box. He slowly stepped down from the ladder. He carried the old box that was falling apart sitting it next to the metal shelving. He opened the box, seeing an old dusty carousel. He smiled seeing it was an older model. He remembered when he was in his second year of secondary education he had made a carousel in science class. All second year students were required to construct a carousel, which was a likeness of the universe. Planets revolving around a sun, with life on the third planet. The sun had to be placed in the center with planets orbiting the sun. The third planet was landscaped with clay then layered with nucleic acids including DNA and RNA, proteins, lipids, and glycans. Which were the building blocks of life creating cells. An atmosphere was pumped in. Water was added, finally flora and fauna including trees. Animals were also formed after the trees were established. Students would study the carousel noting the progress of life in detailed notes. Planets orbiting around the sun seemed to dance as some moved faster as others moved slower. Students would carefully describe in their notes everything occurring inside the glass container.

Carousel's would normally last most of the lunar cycle then would begin to break down with each planet falling and finally life would die out turning to dust. Hal saw the dates were old. They were sixty lunar cycles old.

Hal removed three other boxes sitting them next to the first one. When he grasped the fifth one he realized it was heavier. He removed it carefully, sitting it next to the other four. The old box was falling apart so he reached in taking out the old carousel, seeing it looked much like the others. The outside protective glass was dusty. He wiped the dust away and was surprised to see planets rotating around the sun. He thought this was impossible. The planets could not possibly survive this long. There is no way the old generator could still be working. He thought that sitting it down must have moved the planets. He watched the planets rotating realizing how they were moving in a standard orbit. This was impossible because the small generator could not possibly have lasted more than a lunar cycle.

Hal looked at the viewer then wiped the thick dust off the lenses using the end of his shirt. He peered through the viewer and was shocked to see there was life including people on the planet. He sat back stunned. He had never heard of a carousel with people. He looked again, seeing people in cities, small towns. There were small vehicles moving quickly around cities. Some of them were flying. There appeared to be a whole world of people, animals, flora and fauna. It was impossible. He looked at the name and date seeing it was indeed sixty lunar cycles. He was stunned.

Hal was confused knowing his planet, Praque, had a lunar satellite that orbited once around his planet, making a lunar cycle. His planet with its lunar satellite orbited around their sun in ten lunar cycles, which was a solar cycle. That would mean the old carousel was six solar cycles, which was not possible.

Hal found the cleaning supplies and cleaned the dust off the carousel. He

peered into the viewer of the other four carousels but only found dust. He knew he had found something astounding. It was an enigma and he had to get the carousel to someone who would know what to do with it, and explain how this was even possible. He would take it to Doctor Franklin. He was the head of Physics and Science at the University.

Hal held the carousel tightly, not wanting to drop it. He knew the carousel was built with a leveling device that kept it from rocking when it was picked up. Riding the escalator to the third floor where the Physics and Science classes were held Hal felt the excitement building knowing Doctor Franklin would be shocked with this discovery. He stepped off the escalator and walked to Dr. Franklin's office. His heart was beating fast as he walked down the empty corridor. It would have been crowded with students and professors in the school year.

Hal walked through the open door into the suite of offices where Dr. Franklin's office was located. Several people were in the open area at desks busily working. He saw Sally look up and smile. His heart jumped seeing her. Sallys smile lit up the room. He continued to walk, turning into Dr. Franklin' office. He saw a small table with books on it next to the wall. He sat the carousel on the desk and began taking books off the small table.

"Hey Hal what are you doing? Sally asked surprised.

"I'm cleaning off this table." He said turning and picking up the carousel sitting it on the table.

"Dr. Franklin is very particular about his office. You shouldn't be moving his things!"

Sally had raised her voice.

Hal walked up to her kissing her lightly on the lips. "Where is Dr. Franklin?"

"He's in the gallery talking with some visiting professors. He's scheduled to give a talk on physical science and how it relates to physics. " She said, surprised watching Hal walk out of the room quickly.

Hal did not hesitate. He opened the door to the large gallery that students normally would have been sitting in. It was a large open room with over three hundred seats. Hal saw Dr. Franklin standing near the large platform where the professor would speak. He walked up to him as he was speaking to several other people.

Dr. Franklin, I need to speak to you." Hal blurted out.

Dr. Franklin turned surprised to see Hal who was covered with dust and sweat. "I need to speak with you Dr. Franklin. It's very important." Hal repeated forcefully.

"I'm sure it can wait. I am currently engaged in a conversation, Hal." Dr. Franklin had turned and looked directly at Hal.

Hal stepped closer to Dr. Franklin. "Sir I have found something you will want to see. It is beyond explaining. You have to see it." Hal did not blink as he stared into the eyes of Dr. Franklin.

Dr. Franklin was now irritated. "I'm sure it can wait. I will see you in a little while Hal!"

Hal shook his head. "I apologize for the interruption but you will want to see this sir."

Dr. Franklin turned to the two men and three women, "please excuse me."

He glared at Hal. They both walked out of the gallery.

Stepping on the escalator neither spoke. Hal knew Dr. Franklin was angry. He was no doubt beyond angry. They both walked down the corridor and into his suite of offices. He followed Hal into his office.

"There on the table, the old carousel!" Hal said excitedly.

Dr. Franklin looked at the old carousel. "So what about it? Is this why you so rudely interrupted me? You want me to see an old carousel?"

"Look through the viewer." Hal said just above a whisper.

Dr. Franklin walked to the carousel, bent down and looked through the viewer. He bolted upright, turned and stared at Hal. He turned and looked through the viewer again, seeing cities, small towns, people and animals on every continent. He was shocked. He had seen thousands of carousels. He had been an instructor of Secondary Education science when he graduated from a University. He had taught second year students how to set up a carousel and take notes. He had never in that time seen people.

"What did you do to achieve this Hal?" He asked stunned

"I didn't do anything to the carousel. I was cleaning the basement and I found a door behind some metal shelving. Inside was a closet. The top shelf had five old carousels. The first four were dust. This one is what you see."

Dr. Franklin stood silently looking at Hal. He was speechless. His mind was spinning as he considered all the possibilities. What he was seeing and what Hal was saying was impossible. It went against the laws of physics and science. It was simply not possible for a carousel to evolve into this level of sophistication.

"You are about to be booted out of this University if you don't start telling me the truth. It is not possible for a carousel to evolve to this level. I don't like practical jokes."

"I swear Dr. Franklin I did not tamper with this old carousel. I found it like it is." Hal said, now scared.

Dr. Franklin turned, looking at the old carousel. He could tell it was older. It was older than the ones he had used while teaching. He looked at the name, Anne Hamilton. The date was sixty lunar cycles. He walked to the old machine and saw through the glass the planets rotating. He reached down pushing the lever to raise it up. It did not move. "Hal, come here and grab the glass. I want you to lift up carefully."

Hal walked to the table and grasped the glass lifting slowly. Dr. Franklin pushed on the lever until the scissor lift opened, raising the machine. Dr. Franklin peered at the mechanism. He could see the wiring was what he expected. There was some corrosion on the wires and the small generator. He smiled seeing the old generator. He had not seen one this old for years. It appeared to be running. He pushed down on the lever watching the old carousel move down into position.

"Okay, Hal, let's go to the basement and gather the other machines. I want to inspect them."

Hal and Doctor Franklin made two trips in order to bring the four older carousel's to his office. He had Sally clear off space on the top of a bookshelf so the machines could sit on top. Sally cleaned the machines carefully.

Doctor Franklin inspected each machine thoroughly. The four older carousel's were not different in any way. They appeared to be outdated carousels that were no longer used since the newer models had been improved over the years.

Doctor Franklin sitting behind his desk looked at Hal smiling, "You should go to your dorm and take a shower, Hal. I'm sure when you take Sally out tonight she will want you to be clean for your date."

Hal smiled shyly. He walked toward the door. "Hal," he turned, seeing Dr. Franklin had followed him to the door. "Perhaps you should not say anything about this odd carousel."

"Who would believe me?" he said as he walked out of the office.

# Chapter II

DOCTOR ERIC FRANKLIN sat at his desk looking at the old carousel watching the planets orbiting with their lunar satellites around the sun. His mind was reeling as he considered the possibility of the old carousel lasting as long as sixty lunar cycles. It was just not possible. Laws of physics as he knew did not allow for this type of anomaly. The longest he knew a carousel lasted was approximately a full cycle, and that was rare.

He stood up walking to his file cabinet. He opened the third drawer taking out several wires. With the wires in hand he walked to the carousel placing the wires into the ports of the carousel. He inserted the wires into the ports on his computer. He walked around sitting in his chair and opened the icon on his computer. He began reading the data from the old carousel.

Eric sat back after an hour stunned. It appeared the old carousel had continued to operate after many lunar cycles, which was beyond its lifespan. The flora and fauna with trees then animals had grown as he would have expected. There did not seem to be anything unusual in the beginning of the project. He smiled seeing three of the outer planets were too big. The inner planet closest to the sun was smaller as was the ninth planet furthest from the sun. The seventh planet was at a ninety degree angle. There appeared to be an asteroid belt where a planet had exploded. This sometimes happens if the students' calculations are not accurate. That would account for the two smaller planets. All the planets should have been the same size. Some of the planets had rings circling them. He knew sometimes a lunar satellite or two would explode then orbit around the planet creating a ring. It was due to the students' math not being correct causing the explosion. The student had chosen a standard constellation pattern. Eric was amazed as he saw how the planet had evolved from simple animals to more complex animals. He was shocked to see how people had populated the planet.

He sat back remembering his days of teaching students and the carousel project. He had enjoyed watching as students carefully planned out their own universe. Each of the students had to use math to calculate the distance from the sun for each planet. The size of the planets with lunar satellites orbiting around the planet had to be precise. The third planet would be landscaped and prepared for the atmosphere, water, building blocks of life, then flora and fauna. Simple animals would be introduced on land and in the water. The planets hoovered in place because of gravity which had to be calculated precisely which allowed them to rotate on their axes. Planets would have specific numbers of lunar satellites which orbit at a specific distance and speed. Planets and lunar satellites orbited around the sun. The sun had to have a specific degree of heat or it would be too weak to sustain life. Too hot and it would destroy the atmosphere which would result in the destruction of life on the third planet. It was a fun experiment that taught students physical science and laws of physics. Students would take detailed notes that were stored in the carousel. The carousel had a small computer that also recorded events on the planet, including weather, quakes, eruptions or any anomaly. He had done the same experiment when he was in school. The carousel project had ignited his love for science and physics.

Eric looked at the clock seeing it was late. He stood up and turned off the computer. He looked at the carousel seeing the planets rotating around the sun. He closed his eyes thinking it was just not possible, but he was seeing it with his own eyes. He would have to spend a lot of time studying this enigma.

Eric stepped off the trolly and began walking towards his home. Arriving at the small house, He opened the door seeing his wife Shirley sitting on the couch reading a book. She stood up, obviously upset. He was late again.

Eric smiled. "I was on my way home and stopped at the pub. I met an attractive woman and we started talking. Well one thing led to another and we ended up at her house in bed."

Shirley did not smile. "Stop it Eric! You no doubt had some science project you were working on and lost track of time." She shook her head walking into the kitchen. Eric followed her. Shirley picked up a large platter of food, taking it to the table. "It's cold, I reheated it but you are of course late. I really try to prepare a good meal for you but you always get tangled up in some project." She sat down looking at Eric. "And then tell some ridiculous story about a woman in the pub."

Eric filled his plate. "Well it could happen."

Shirley laughed, "No, if a woman was to come on to you in an aggressive way. You would turn and run out the door." She laughed. "You were so shy I had to ask you out, lover boy."

Eric's face turned blue. "Well I did get caught up in a project. It is beyond anything I have seen, or even heard of. An old carousel was found in the basement by an undergraduate. We need the basement for a lab. Anyway the carousel was still working after six solar cycles. And it has evolved to where it has people on the planet."

Shirley stared at Eric. She sat her fork down. "You expect me to believe a carousel, which second year students created, lasted six solar cycles, and it has evolved to have people on the planet" She picked up her fork. "I would believe the story of you picking up a floozy than that whopper of a tale."She said laughing.

"I know it's wild. But somehow this carousel has lasted six solar cycles. I can't explain it. I'll show it to you tomorrow."

"The University is closed, it's the weekend," Shirley said, reaching for her glass of water.

"I know that's why I will show you when no one else is around. It is incredible."

They sat quietly for a while when Shirley, who was curious, asked. "Eric, are you serious about this old carousel? You expect me to believe that a carousel project can really last six solar cycles?"

"No, I don't expect you to believe it. That is why we are going to my office tomorrow when no one is around so you can experience it for yourself."

The following morning Shirley followed Eric into his office. She saw his office was neat and tidy, everything in its place. Eric pointed to the old carousel sitting on a small table. She walked to it looking into the viewer. She was shocked to see humanoid people inside the carousel. She moved the knob zooming in seeing the small people were different . She was surprised to see lighter skinned people and darker skinned people. The people were of different sizes and lived on the entire planet. She stood up "what did you do to create this world? Is this a hologram?"

"That's just it, I didn't do anything. It was found just like you see it. I did go to the basement and examined other projects it was found with. They are all dust as you would expect. They do not appear to be any different than this one."

Shirley looked at the name. "This Anne Hamilton must have done something to change the parameters."

"If she did I can't find how she did it. The data shows she did everything as she was supposed to. Her notes do not indicate anything different. Looking through her notes I'm not sure she was a great student. I'm not being critical but as a teacher it appears she didn't do real well in class. She seems to have struggled with math and science. I would guess she was an average student."

Shirley sat down in the chair in front of Eric's desk. This was unbelievable. Her project in school has lasted for most of the cycle. All of the projects had eventually died out. Even the brightest students couldn't keep the project going. "How is this possible Eric?"

"I don't know. It defies logic, the laws of physics and science. There is no way the small generator should be working this long. I have no idea how people were created on this carousel."

Neither one of them spoke. Shirley, who worked in the legal council's office for many lunar cycles and had been recently appointed as Judge, thought of the project. She looked at Eric. "What are the legal implications?"

Eric looked surprised. "Why would there be legal issues? This is a project for a second year student?"

Shirley smiled. "Oh honey there will no doubt be legal complications. There could be a claim of fraud. Perhaps trying to mislead the public. I suggest you study this and we should do some preliminary investigation before you reveal this to the world."

"I don't think it will be anything like that Shirley. It's an anomaly."

Shirley stood up, "Lets talk with Anne Hamilton. It is possible she is still living. We will see if she did anything unique. I believe this could be bigger than just a science project."

She kissed Eric on the cheek. "Don't stay too late. I'll have supper ready at six."

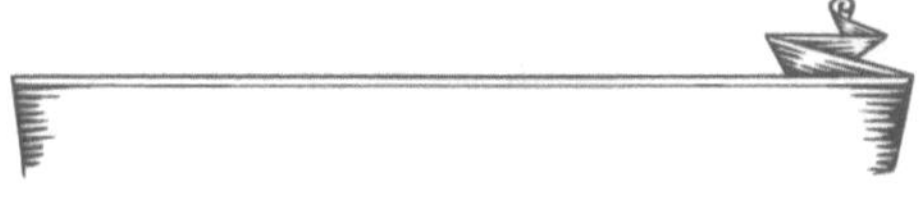

# Chapter III

Eric arrived home at seven thirty. Shirley looked up from her book. She stood up, turning going into the kitchen. "We're having sandwiches and chips."

Eric smiled, "my favorite."

"Careful, or you will have it every night. So what have you been able to discover about this new world recently discovered?" Shirley asked as she sat the food on the table.

"Interesting," Eric said as he began making a sandwich. "As you recall from your days in secondary education, the third planet has life on it. The satellite that orbits the planet is larger than it should be. There was a mistake in the students' math. The humanoid people call the lunar satellite a moon. Anyway the moon rotates quickly around the planet in a thirty day cycle as opposed to a full year as ours does. Again a mistake in calculation. So for the people on the planet their time would be calculated to hundreds of thousands of cycles, while for us it has been sixty lunar cycles or years. Also, the student chose to have ten planets as is sometimes done. However, a planet exploded when the generator was started and created an asteroid belt. For some reason the asteroid belt did not disintegrate as it usually does. It continues to rotate around the sun as it would have as a planet. The same with some of the smaller lunar satellites or moons as they refer to that orbit a planet. One or two exploded causing the debris to form rings that circle the planet. There are so many anomalies in the project." Eric sat quietly eating. He looked at Shirley, "I cannot find in the data when the humanoid people show up. What is intriguing, is when the planet was forming there were many different species of humanoid people. They were different from each other, but in many ways similar. It is interesting how they began to merge together. Some of the humanoid species die off or were absorbed into another species of humanoids. There appears to be only one set of the humanoid species now, called homosapiens, but they are a mixture of many of the other species of humanoid from the past."

Shirley held up her hand, "hold it Eric, you're confusing me. What do you mean different species? They are humanoid people."

Eric smiled. "Yes they are humanoid. Studying the data from the computer there were some species called, Homo habilis, Home rudolfensis, Homo erectus, Homo antecessor, Homo heidecessor, and others. These humanoid people developed in the ancient past. They were similar to homo sapiens, but were a different species. "

"So the ancient ancestors from different species could interbreed. That doesn't make sense." Shirley said, looking at Eric.

"No, perhaps not, I'm not sure I understand how different species can interbreed, but they did." Eric said smiling. "I'll keep studying this anomaly."

"Okay, so explain to me Doctor Franklin why are the people different colors?"

Shirley asked as she ate.

"There are different races. I believe that would be more appropriate than colors. I'm not sure how they evolved into different races when they are all of the same humanoid species. They often intermarry within the races. I'm not sure at this point." Eric was lost in his thoughts then continued. "They have established governments, religions, educational systems, and monetary systems in their cultures. Humanoid species occupy all areas of the planet but have different cultures, with different viewpoints. There have been wars over these differences but there is also peace." He looked at Shirley. "They are a complex society."

"So why are there different races? Why is our society only one color, oh I'm sorry Doctor, race, when we are all pale blue. Why are they not like us?"

Eric smiled. "They are pretty people, like you my dear."

Shirley raised her hand, shaking her finger. "Too late for you to be charming, you're still in trouble for being late. Answer the question Doctor."

Eric laughed. "Okay Judge Shirley. Like I stated earlier. I don't know how they were introduced into the carousel. I'm not sure how the animals have become complex from the simple animals that were first introduced by the student. The people just seem to have appeared. The animals evolved. They appear and reproduce. Over time in their own microcosm the humanoid people began to develop complex societies over the cycles. Their government evolved, as did their religion. Some cultures believed in multiple Gods, then over time they began to change their beliefs to believing in only one God or the belief in no God."

Shirley stopped eating, She wiped her mouth. "Did you say no God? You mean they don't believe in God?"

Eric shrugged his shoulders, "Some of the people in the carousel don't believe there is a God. Most do believe. God to the people has different names depending on where the people are located, but I believe it is the same God. The difference is he is worshiped in a different way with different traditions."

"That's ridiculous, of course there is a God, and only one." Shirley said, sitting back. "Sounds like they're stupid."

Eric smiled. "No, I believe there is intelligence in the people in the carousel. You have been raised to believe in our God. So it doesn't make sense if someone doesn't believe as you do."

"Hold on Eric, are you calling me ignorant? There is one God who created the universe and all the other planets and creatures on them." Shirley was furious.

Eric held up his hand "easy Judge, I'm not questioning your faith, or beliefs. I'm just saying the people in the carousel have a choice, and it is their choice to believe or worship as they chose. Also most of the humanoid people believe they are the only people, no other people exist outside their planet. In some ways they are correct. They are the only ones in their galaxy. They have no idea there is a larger world outside their small galaxy."

"So Eric, how do you know so much about their culture?"

"They keep detailed records. Their languages are different from ours. I was able to translate their languages with artificial intelligence.

They sat quietly eating each lost in their own thoughts. After a while Shirley said, "Oh by the way I have found Anne Hamilton. The lady who constructed the carousel."

Eric was surprised "Wow that was fast. How did you track her down so fast? There may be more than one Anne Hamilton."

Shirley smiled as she picked up the food, clearing the table. "I work in the legal field. It's my job to get the right suspect."

Eric laughed, "suspect, she's not a suspect."

Shirley walked to the living room sitting down on a small sofa. Eric sat next to her. "Okay listen up Doctor. The old carousel was found in the basement of the University. It is sixty lunar cycles old. Six solar cycles ago Northwestern University was a secondary education school. Northwestern took control and opened for business as a higher education University twenty lunar cycles ago. A student named Anne Hamilton attended the secondary school. She is the only Anne Hamilton enrolled and to graduate from the school called North Central. It is called that because it is in the north central part of the city. Are you still with me honey? Are you keeping up? Okay then, North Central was shut down twenty lunar cycles ago because of the smaller number of students. It was the same time many people decided to go off world to Samoa which is a planet that had large agriculture opportunities. So Anne graduated, went into her two year mandatory military service. She stayed twenty five lunar cycles. When she retired she then worked in civil service in law enforcement for another twenty five lunar cycles then retired, with two retirements. She lives in Sunnydale district. Which is a community set aside for elderly folks. We can go see her tomorrow after church."

Eric smiled, "you were able to find out all this information in one afternoon."

"You know before being named a Judge, I was an attorney. I spent a lot of time tracking down people who were reluctant to come to court. It's what I do." Shirley sat back "you impressed?"

"Yes I am. I'm impressed with myself, I got beauty and brains with you."

Shirley smiled, "No, you just got lucky."

# Chapter IV

IT WAS RAINING WHEN Eric and Shirley walked out of church. The rain came every afternoon. The congregation opened their umbrellas as they made their way to their vehicles.

The planet Praque was a large planet that consisted of four continents and mostly water. The sun was obscured most of the time by large clouds. Prague was the fifth planet in the solar system and colder than the other two planets which were inhabited. The people of Praque had a pale light blue complexion, light blue/white hair and blue, or hazel eyes. The third and forth planets were also inhabited with people having lighter red/brown skin, dark hair, and dark eyes.

Eric and Shirley stepped onto the trolly that moved quickly around the large city of Pharm. They stepped off in the arts district for lunch. When they finished lunch they walked a few blocks to the older neighborhood of Sunnydale since the sun had broken through the clouds.

Sunnydale was the oldest part of town and had been established as a retirement village. The houses were smaller, consisting of mostly two or three bedrooms. It had been mostly a working class neighborhood when it was first built, but had fallen into disrepair when many people moved to Samoa. The city of Phram had repaired the older houses allowing the growing number of retirees to move in.

Shirley pointed to a small house with a small yard with beautiful flowers growing in front of a small porch. A small older lady was sitting on an old metal chair on the old porch. She watched as the couple walked up the sidewalk.

Shirley smiled broadly as she walked up the old wooden steps. "Elder Hamilton?"

The older woman stood up slowly. She wore a simple yellow dress with two large pockets in the front. Her hair was snow white, her skin was a very light blue. Her blue eyes seemed to sparkle as she smiled. "Yes, I'm Anne Hamilton."

Shirley placed her small hand on the older woman's face showing respect. "We don't mean to intrude but would like to speak to you if it is convenient."

Her hand stayed on the cheek for a while then Shirley slowly dropped it. Anne was surprised and pleased at the old custom of greeting an elder. It had seemed to have been used less and less over the years. "I would be pleased to have you sit and talk. Would you mind if we sit outside? It is such a beautiful day."

Shirley smiled, "I would like that Elder Hamilton." She stepped back with her head slightly lowered. "May I introduce my husband Doctor Eric Franklin."

Eric stepped close to Anne placing his hand on her cheek. "I am pleased to meet you, Elder Hamilton. My wife Shirley Franklin, Judge of the city of Phram."

Anne smiled broadly knowing the introductions were formal. "Please have a seat."

Eric pulled up two of the old metal chairs. They had recently been painted yellow. He sat down after Shirley sat down. Anne looked at the two guests with curiosity wondering why two prestigious people would pay her a visit.

Shirley who was always gracious and handled conversations so casually spoke first. "I love your house Elder Hamilton. It has personality."

"Thank you I moved in almost seven lunar cycles when I retired from Halifax. I love the house. I have been busy since my husband has passed."

I regret your loss. I pray the Lord has brought you comfort." Shirley said softly.

"It is good to see such manors, I pray the Lord blesses you." Anne said, smiling.

Eric sat quiet knowing that formal introductions were important. Most people had abandoned the formality of meeting an elder thinking it was old fashioned. He leaned forward slightly. "Elder Hamilton we have come because of a unique situation that has arisen. I am head of the Physics and Science division at Northwestern University. Recently a carousel has been found in the basement. I believe it is yours when you were in your second year of secondary school would you tell me about the project."

Anne sat quite not sure why such a question was asked. She smiled then laughed softly. "Well, Doctor Franklin, I was not a very good student. I was average. Math and Sciences did not come easily. My Father spent many hours trying to explain the work I brought home. I found the carousel project difficult." she sat quietly then asked, "Why would you ask about a project I received a barely passing grade on?"

"I ask, because it is still running," Eric said matter of factly.

Shirley rolled her eyes and stared at Eric. He of course was brilliant but had no tact. She looked quickly at Anne who sat shocked. "I realize it is hard to comprehend how a simple project could still be operating after so many years. I assure you the carousel you constructed is still running." She looked at Eric, her eyes flashing with anger. "Perhaps you should try a little tact Eric!" Her voice was low and forceful.

Eric was surprised as he looked at his wife. He took a deep breath. "I didn't mean to be rude. I am simply stating a fact. The carousel is still running."

"You could have made your statement less rude. I would have expected you to work up to this fact rather than blurting it out." Shirley's voice was still low.

"I was honest, and saw no need to waste time in a frivolous manner, and I was not rude."

"You were rude, and blunt. Courtesy is not frivolous, Eric!" Shirley said, raising her voice."

"I was polite to Elder Hamilton. Being straight forward is not rude. Perhaps you should not be so critical, Judge Franklin!"

Shirley setup straight leaning forward. Her eyes flashing anger, "careful Doctor Franklin how you talk to me. I'm not one of your students to bully. You are about to walk into an area you won't find pleasant."

The two stared at each other when Anne said quietly. "Perhaps we should have some refreshments." Anne stood up slowly using the arms on her chair to assist her. Shirley stood up as well.

"I will help you." She looked sternly at Eric. "That would be courteous."

Eric watched the two women walk into the house.

The two women walked out of the house a short time later, Anne carrying a plate of small cakes. Shirley handed Eric a glass of ade which was a berry from a tree growing in Anne's back yard. He smiled, taking the glass and a small cake.

Sitting down, the group was quiet. "This is good," Eric said as he took another bite of the cake.

"It's my mothers recipe. I believe it is the best cake in the galaxy." Anne said as she watched the couple.

"May I ask Doctor Franklin, how is it possible for a carousel to be still running after all these cycles?"

Eric wiped his mouth with a small napkin. "I don't know. I truly don't know how it is possible for a project so long ago is continuing." He hesitated then said carefully picking his words, "the project seems to have evolved."

"How so?" Anne asked, looking directly at Eric.

Eric smiled nervously. "The carousel has evolved over the cycles. The fauna and flowers with trees have continued to develop and thrive. Animals with humanoid people have also appeared. It is a sophisticated microcosm world."

"I don't see how that is possible, Doctor Franklin." Anne said, surprised.

Eric asked "will you tell me about the project Elder Hamilton?"

Anne sat quietly then spoke. "I was an average student. In the second year at North Central, Elder Foghart was the instructor. He was an elderly man who had taught the class for many solar cycles. We were told to pick out a carousel which we did. He handed out a single sheet of paper with the instructions, or parameters as he called it for completing the project. I struggled with the math aligning the planets with gravity including rotating on their axis and orbiting around the sun. I was nervous about the math because of the heat of the sun. I did ask for help after class and my classmates did offer help. I could not ask for help during class because it was not a group project, and with Elder Foghart constantly watching I struggled by myself.

I chose to have seven continents on the third planet. Some students chose five. It was difficult landscaping the planet. The clay would get too hard, or it was soft and slipped off the planet. After the first quarter Elder Foghart placed the generator under the carousel and started it." Anne giggled softly. "He frowned at my project because the planets were not the same size, and the seventh planet tilted ninety degrees. One of the planets I believe was the fifth planet exploded. He said the third planet was too close to the sun and it wobbled. My calculations were off, and it would destroy the atmosphere. He was surprised when at the end of the lunar cycle it was still running. I remember inputting the data everyday watching the planet grow and change. At the end of the year all of the projects had died and turned to dust. He placed mine in a box saying, "It will stop in a few days." I received a passing grade but only average. Elder Fogheart was not pleased with my effort. Bobby Horton and I took the carousels to the basement. We placed them all in the closet for next year's students."

Anne stopped talking as she remembered the past. She looked at Shirley "I graduated with average grades. I served my time in the military, and liked it so much I stayed. I was stationed on the planet Alex where I met my husband Doug. He was a botanist. I was an instructor in the military. We married and were together for sixty five lunar cycles." She sat quietly. Then continued. "We moved to Halifax when I retired from the military. Doug helped terraform the planet. I worked in law enforcement. It was exciting. We left after twenty five lunar cycles then moved home." A tear formed in Anne's eyes as she thought of her husband.

"Did you grow up here?" Shirley asked.

Anne smiled, wiping her eyes. "Yes," She pointed to the end of the block. "That two story house on the corner is where my home was many cycles ago. At that time there were lots of families and so many children. I went to Chandler Prime, then to North Central Secondary. I didn't attend a University because of my grades. The military was a good place for me. I have no regrets."

Eric sat contemplating what he had heard. Anne was an average student. What could have caused the carousel to continue running? How could life be created from her project?

"I am at a loss Doctor Franklin how or why the project I had six solar cycles could be running. I followed the parameters the best I could. I suppose you should consult the church elders. Perhaps the Lord has intervened."

Eric, and Shirley stayed and talked with Anne for another hour then left for home.

# Chapter V

ERIC WOULD SPEND THE break studying the strange humanoid life forms as well as the animals that had been created over the sixty lunar cycles within the carousel. Shirley would often go to the University to take Eric his supper since he would often lose track of time. He had become obsessed with the project.

One evening as like many others Shirley walked into Eric's office seeing him staring into the viewer of the carousel. Holding the plate in her hand said "I brought you supper honey. I'm not sure how a person can forget to eat?"

Eric looked up, his tired eyes showed the strain of working late. "Thank you Shirley. I guess I have been working a lot lately."

Shirley sat the plate on his desk as Eric stood up and stretched. He walked to his chair behind his desk and sat down. Shirley sat quiet as she watched him eat. She took a deep breath letting it out slowly. "So, have you discovered how the humanoid people with complex societies were created?"

Eric shook his head. "It's a mystery, I'm not sure if the DNA, and RNA created a cell that over time mutated into human form."

"Is that how our race was created by mutating DNA and RNA?" Shirley asked, looking directly at Eric.

Eric smiled, "No, you know the Lord created our race and those across the galaxy. We are different, but our religion is specific. We have a soul."

"Do the small humanoid people in the carousel have a soul?" she asked.

Eric had his fork halfway to his mouth. He stopped and looked at Shirley. She leaned forward looking directly at him. "Well, do they have a soul, Doctor Franklin?"

Eric sat back looking at Shirley. "Am I being cross examined, Judge Franklin?"

"Just answer the question, Doctor. Do the small inhabitants in the carousel have a soul? Do they believe they have a soul? Didn't you state they have a religion and believe in God. They believe according to their religion they have a soul, and will go to heaven when they die."

"What is this all about Shirley? Why are you treating me like I'm on trial? This is an experiment that an average second year student constructed six solar cycles ago. It is an enigma."

Shirley leaned forward looking at Eric. "Anne said she was in civil service, law enforcement on the planet Halifax. That was a rough planet. Your Father and Mother, and my Father were stationed there after it was terraformed. That barron rock with little vegetation was transformed into a beautiful lush planet. If you recall there were inhabitants that had lived there for eons. Once the planet was transformed, colonists from here and other planets moved there. Our religious sector demanded the Halifax people stop worshiping nature. The native Halifax people believed all nature was alive and had a soul. Our religious order demanded they stop worshiping creation and worship the creator. Our military had to go in and put down a rebellion. Years later they sued in court for their right to worship as they chose. I was on the team." Shirley sat back as her voice broke with emotion. Tears spilled from her eyes running down her cheek. "I was a young attorney that went to Halifax and we won in court.

The native Halifax people could not worship as they had for many solar cycles. There are people who are arrested to this day because they refuse to worship as they are being forced to do. We won the case for our religious sector and our government. It doesn't feel like a victory." Shirley sat quiet looking down at her hands. "I regret being part of the team that robbed them of their right to worship as they had for eons."

Eric remembered he was in a boarding school when his parents were called up for military duty. There were several battles on Halifax. The natives were defeated but they continued to worship in underground churches. His Father and Mother said it was a disgrace to have been in battle with people forced to submit to a rigid religious order.

Shirley said quietly. "Eric you need to understand there could and most likely will be a lot of controversy over this project. I know the law, and have seen the ugly side of politics and religious extremists. You need to be prepared in case it gets ugly."

Eric sat quietly listening. "Do you think it will go that far? It is an experiment that has some anomalies. It's science, I think you are making this out to be a bigger deal than it is honey."

Shirley smiled. "I hope you are right. I will start preparing just in case it goes too far." she stood up, "so when will you reveal this to the rest of the population. I hope you have a good presentation prepared."

"I will talk to Doctor Sanford after the weekend. He is a reasonable man and he will present this when he is ready."

Shirley stood up. "Sounds like a plan." She walked to the door, turned and looked at Eric. "Don't stay too late. Also tell Doctor Sanford you have a good attorney." She smiled "and you sleep with her."

# Chapter VI

DOCTOR ROGER SANFORD looked up from his desk seeing Eric walk in with an old carousel with a young man following him carrying a small table. The young man sat the table next to Roger's desk as Eric sat the carousel on top of it.

Eric said "Thank you Hal."

Hal nodded to Roger then left the room. Eric sat in a chair across from Roger.

"So what can I do for you Eric? I understand you have an urgent matter to discuss." Roger looked at the old carousel on the table. "I haven't seen an old carousel like this for years. It looks like one I would have used in my second year of secondary school."

Eric was nervous. "Yes Doctor Sanford I have an odd development that has recently come up." He hesitated, taking a breath. "What I am about to tell you, you will not believe. You are correct that the carousel is old. That is why I am here." He sat quietly thinking how he should start.

"Well Eric you have my attention, please enlighten me, I am curious."

Eric began telling Roger how the carousel was found, how it was running after six solar cycles. He explained how He and Shirley had spoken with Anne Hamilton who was the student who had constructed the carousel. The strange anomalies that had occurred since it had continued to run over the cycles. The appearance of humanoid people who had developed complex societies. When he finished he stood up handing Roger a disk "this has all my data collected."

Roger reached up taking the disk he placed it in his computer and began reading the information. After a while he stood up going to the carousel. He stared at it watching the planets orbiting then slowly leaned down looking through the viewer. He zoomed in using the small knobs turned them so he could see all parts of the world inside the carousel. He stood up walking to his desk sitting down. He was quiet for some time and looked up "I have to say I am stunned. This is more than unbelievable; it is beyond words. This defies all laws of physics and science. We may have to reconsider what we believe."

Both men sat quietly, each lost in their own thoughts. Eric cleared his throat, "Doctor Sanford, my wife Shirley is a Judge as you know. She is of the opinion that this could cause controversy."

"She's right. I have no doubt this will cause a sensation. We will need to handle this delicately." Roger leaned back in his chair considering all the possibilities. He sat up, "the carousel was found in the basement. My wife Betsy attended secondary school here when it was North Central. She would be about the same age as Anne Hamilton. She may know her. Perhaps she could give us some insight on her. Maybe shed some light on this anomaly as you refer to it."

Roger dialed his home and placed the phone on speaker. A pleasant voice answered the phone. "Hello, Sanford residence."

"Betsy, I hope I'm not disturbing you. I have you on speaker, Doctor Eric Franklin is with me. Do you have time to talk?"

"Yes of course dear. I know Doctor Franklin, his pretty wife is a Judge. Do you think he could speak to her for me? I received a citation by a rather rude law enforcement officer for, as he claimed, "exceeding the speed limit" when I clearly was not."

"No, dear I don't think that would be appropriate. You were no doubt speeding since you have received numerous citations in the past. I'm calling to ask about when you attended secondary education at North Central."

"I was not speeding, and the officer was rude. I don't believe it would be inappropriate for Doctor Franklin to mention it to his wife. What was it, you ask North Central? Yes I am a proud graduate of old North Central. We were mostly a working class neighborhood, not a snooty elite school. Oh I meant no offense dear since you went to an elite school."

Roger smiled. "Do you remember a student, Anne Hamilton?"

"Anne Hamilton! Yes we were friends. She lived on the corner of Yale. That was directly behind my house. She was a lot of fun. Her Father worked in the assayer's office. Her Mother was a baker in the school. She made the best cinnamon rolls."

"Was she a good student?"

Betsy laughed. "No, she was average at best. She was a great athlete and a great cook. Why do you ask Honey?"

"Do you recall in your second year, the carousel project? How, did Anne do with her carousel?"

"Well that's certainly odd. I remember we were all excited about the project. Old High Pockets was such a grouchy old man. We called him high pockets because he wore his pants pulled up so far he could reach over his shoulder and take out his wallet!" Betsy began laughing.

Roger sat back shaking his head. "Could you please stay on track dear. You seem to have wandered from the subject. Please try to stay focused."

Betsy was still laughing. "Okay dear don't get grumpy. Anne struggled with the math and getting her planets aligned and rotating. One of her planets blew up, and one tilted to where it was almost on its side. Old Foggy frowned saying her project would not last a quarter of the cycle. He was surprised it was still running at the end of the lunar cycle."

Roger let his breath out slowly. "I would appreciate it, Betsy, if you showed more respect when referring to your late instructor. Did Anne do anything special? Like adding chemicals or anything to the project?"

"No, Elder Fogheart being the instructor was the only one who could put in the atmosphere. He supervised each student when the building block chemicals were added. It was supervised closely by Foggy, oh excuse me Doctor Sanford Elder Fogheart."

Betsy began to laugh as it was obvious Roger was getting frustrated.

"Why are you so interested in Anne? You know she lives in Sunnydale. I had lunch with her and some other friends a few weeks ago. You know she retired from the military and law enforcement in Halifax. That's a rough neighborhood. She has two retirements!"

"Do you remember if anything was different about her carousel project?" Roger asked patiently.

"No, we were all surprised Anne's carousel ran as long as it did. Several people helped her after class, since Foggy kept saying "this is not a group project. You need to pay attention to your own carousel!" Betsy laughed. "You know Anne could do great impressions. We were in gym class and the instructor wasn't there. She started doing an impression of high pockets and the head chancellor Perkins. It was hilarious. Well Perkins came in and he was mad when he saw Anne doing her impression of him. He made us all run the rest of the hour!" Betsy was laughing hysterically.

Roger let his breath out, "Okay honey thank you. You were no help."

"Now that is just rude Roger. Anne was a good student, she did struggle but her carousel did keep running after some of the smart alec boys who thought they were the brains of the class had stopped. I know Anne and Bobby Horton took all the carousel's to the basement, so they could be used next year. Anne said Bobby kissed her while they were in the basement."

"I'll see you tonight Betsy."

"So will you ask Doctor Franklin to speak to his wife about my citation?"

"No." Roger hung up.

Roger leaned back in his chair. After a short while he sat up and smiled, "I married an artist. You know she may be a bit goofy as all artists are, she is entertaining."

Eric tried not to laugh. "We did learn one thing. Anne did not tamper with the project. There is no evidence anybody did. Somehow it sat in the basement closet for six solar cycles and somehow evolved into a sophisticated society."

Roger dropped his smile. "I believe your wife is correct. This may be very controversial. I believe we should present the findings to the Education Board of Directors next week. The meeting will be a few days prior to the first day of school. I need you to present this to the board. I'll let you know more when I figure out exactly how we will handle this."

# Chapter VII

ERIC SAT IN THE AUDIENCE next to Shirley. He was nervous about giving a presentation to the board. Doctor Sanford had met with him wanting to hear of his presentation. Roger was pleased with the presentation. He approved of Eric using pictures he had taken of the inhabitants of the carousel. He smiled saying, "a slide show was rather old fashioned, but he thought it was a good idea. He also wanted the old carousel on a table in the room. The board members would no doubt want to see for themselves how the carousel evolved.

The board members were all elders. The five board members were appointed by the Education committee which was a government agency. Marion Higsby was a former chancellor of an elite University, Gaven Acres, was also an educator who had served on the government board for the Education committee, Horace Billings, was a University instructor who had also served as an executive of finance for his University, Robin Myers had also been an educator in the Primary, Secondary, and University instructor, Brenda Norwitch, was a retired Representative in the government, she had represented the elite communities on Prague. The Government consisted of a House of Representatives that represented different areas of the Planet. The Government had Judicial, Legislative, Executive, branches with many committees responsible for running the planet.

Brenda was from a wealthy family. She had pushed for Doctor Sanford to retire for many years. Her son-in-law Burrell Leafton was the Head Finance Director at the University. She wanted him to take over for Roger.

When the board was seated Roger stood up walking to the lectern. He welcomed the board, and spoke of the new year which had an increase of students. He introduced Doctor Eric Franklin and an exciting discovery that had recently been uncovered.

Eric walked to the lectern, and began explaining the discovery of the old carousel. He reported how the carousel which was sixty lunar cycles old had continued to run. He explained how the project had evolved. The pictures on the screen stunned the board as well as the audience.

Journalists were in attendance. They had expected the same routine board meeting with the number of students, faculty, and budgets. They were stunned hearing Eric's presentation.

Eric went into detail explaining the complex society of the humanoid people. How over the cycles they had progressed with their technology and level of sophistication. When he finished the screen went dark. Roger immediately stood up saying "thank you Doctor Franklin for your presentation."

Eric walked to his seat sitting next to Shirley.

The room was silent as all in attendance sat contemplating what they had just seen. It was not possible what they had heard and seen.

Brenda Norwitch's face had turned a deep shade of blue. She was visibly upset.

"Do you expect this board to believe any of the lies Doctor Franklin has presented! I demand his immediate resignation! Doctor Franklin has created this stunt for his own ego!"

Roger remained calm, "the information is in your folders. I realize this information is incredible, and hard to accept. Yet the facts are clear.

Nothing has been fabricated. You are welcome to view the old carousel that is here."

Marion Higsby who was the chairman of the board immediately stood up going to the carousel. He was followed by the others except Brenda. He looked into the viewer and moved the knobs inspecting the inhabitants on the planet. He stepped back as each of the other board members looked through the viewer.

Journalists were on their feet swarming Eric. Roger walked to them saying "please hold your question until after the board meeting. Let's not turn this meeting into chaos which is unprofessional."

The journalist walked back to the chairs.

The board members soon took their seats. Marion was shocked he cleared his throat. "This is not possible, it, it can not happen. How do you explain how a carousel sixty lunar cycles old with older components, and humanoid people evolve into, well into a society that is complex?"

"We can not explain it, Elder Chairman. Doctor Franklin is studying this project, and has not been able to find a satisfactory conclusion." Roger had stayed calm as he spoke.

"Because he lied! This is a hoax and I demand you shut this project down immediately!" Brenda raised her voice, becoming hysterical.

"No." Roger calmly stared at Brenda.

"No! Did you say no? You are refusing a direct order from me, a board member?"

Roger stood quietly then raised his voice "You have no authority to order me to comply with your ridiculous request. This board serves as an oversight committee. I answer to Doctor Ringling, the head of the Education committee."

Brenda was on her feet. "You will not speak to me in such a manner, Doctor Sandford!"

"I realize being a former Representative you believe you have special authority, but you are a board member. You do not instruct me on how I chose to run this University! The carousel is an enigma that is beyond our known physics and laws of science as we understand them. If you had any experience in education, which you do not, you would understand that. The carousel will remain running and Doctor Franklin will continue to examine it, Elder Nortwitch."

Brenda stood with her fists clenched as her face turned a deeper blue. No one had ever spoken so sharply to her and she was offended. The board was surprised since Roger had never spoken to any board member in such a way.

Marion gathered himself saying, "please have a seat Elder Norwich. Doctor Sanford, I would ask you to show more respect to this board. What are your intentions with this project?"

"I meant no disrespect Elder Chairman. If I have offended the board I sincerely apologize. My intention is to study this anomaly. I would welcome other scholars from Universities to come and also study it."

Horace sat staring at Roger. "I believe it would have been more appropriate to have shared this with the board in private as opposed to surprising us with this project."

"With respect Elder It was my intention to share this discovery with everyone. It was not my intention to hide the project from the public." Roger said calmly.

Horace's face turned blue, "are you suggesting this board would have kept this from the public!"

"Yes." Roger said, looking back at the board.

"I am offended and find your lack of confidence in this board disturbing Doctor Sanford." Robin stated calmly.

"I have confidence in this board. I am concerned the board would have wanted to keep it from the public until it felt the time was right. I am not sure the time would have ever been right, and this incredible discovery would have remained secluded."

No one spoke they were shocked this was certainly out of character for Roger. He had always talked with them if there was a sensitive subject or perhaps problem with the University.

Marion said "we can continue with this later. I believe we should move on."

Brenda said loudly, "Elder Chairman I have a concern with Doctor Sanford and the budget. As you are aware Doctor Sanford informed this board of a research project Doctor Franklin was working on that would assist hospitals across this planet and patients as well. He stated this research project would help hospitals save lives by assisting the body to heal itself as opposed to costly medication. I would like to know why the University is in debt as opposed to making a profit as he claimed."

"The program and the discoveries by Doctor Franklin have indeed worked as well as expected. Hospitals across the planet have paid a nominal fee for the research project. This University chose to charge a small fee as opposed to an outrageous fee as some Elite Universities have done. This University has made a tremendous profit. The information concerning the project is in your folder."

Brenda was stunned, she looked through the folder finding at the bottom of the paperwork the budget and the results were indeed astounding.

Roger turned to look at Burrell, who looked shocked. Roger had told him only a few days ago how the project was losing money. When he had asked for information his assistant Beth Cannon said she was still gathering data as it was coming in. He was irritated at Beth for not having information about the project. He reported to Brenda about the program with details Roger had given him. He had been talking to Brenda for years concerning finances of the University.

Roger turned to look at Brenda. "Do you have any more questions, Elder?"

Brenda was furious. "I would like to know how this profit will be spent?"

"Scholarships for students without the financial means to attend a University."

"Ridiculous, the money could be better spent." Brenda stopped speaking, realizing her statement could be perceived wrong. Being a politician she knew better than to blurt out her true feelings.

"Why is that?" Robin asked as she leaned forward looking directly at Brenda.

"I believe we as a board should consider the finances of this facility and offer scholarships to not only underprivileged students, but also pursue the brightest students as well." Brenda said calmly.

"We have scholarships for that. We have been fortunate to have Doctor Sanford who has brought in many of the top students from secondary education. Do you have an issue with students without sufficient funds attending this University?"

"Of course not. I welcome all students. I just want to be sure a proper system is in place."

"That information is also in your packet Elder. The profits from Doctor Franklin's program will benefit not only scholarships, but allow for a raise for faculty. We will also add to our savings account." Roger said without emotion.

The board would vote on the scholarships after discussion approving it. The rest of the board meeting fell into its usual routine. It was adjourned three hours later.

# Chapter VIII

THE JOURNALIST SURROUNDED Eric, all of them asking questions at the same time when the meeting was over. Roger had anticipated the chaos and immediately walked to where Eric and Shirley were surrounded by journalists.

He smiled broadly, "People please you are all making a spectacle of yourselves. All of you speaking at once this is ridiculous. My assistant has given all of you information covering Doctor Franklin's presentation. There is nothing else to add." Roger, taking Eric's arm, and Shirley's hand walked through the mob of reporters.

A young woman went to Brenda asking "Why do you believe it is ridiculous to offer scholarships to students who don't have the funds to attend a University?"

"You're being ridiculous. My comment was aimed at Doctor Sanford, who did not have the professionalism to understand he should have talked to the board first. Informing all of us of the University's finances." She was angry and tried to control her words.

"Oh I believe I heard you correctly Elder. You don't believe Students who are not elite are as bright so they should stay in their class and work for those like you." The young journalist asked smugly.

Brenda took a deep breath, "who do you work for young lady?"

"The Praque Crier, my editor is Josh McClain. I believe you know him well." She said, smiling sweetly.

Brenda walked off quickly. She knew the editor well. He was an enemy against those who were elite. He constantly railed against the elite class and how they pressured Representatives to ensure they were not inconvenienced. She despised him and his paper.

When Eric and Shirley arrived at home. Eric sat down thinking about the carousel. He would wait until tomorrow to study the project. There would also be his responsibilities with the beginning of classes. He was thinking of all he had to do when he heard Shirley say. "Eric, you need to concentrate on gathering data from the carousel. Don't worry about any distractions. I will take care of any issues that come up."

Eric looked at Shirley confused, "I really think you are overreacting. We both knew that when the public was made aware of this strange phenomena there would be a lot of excitement."

Shirley raised her eyebrows, "excitement, oh, my dear when this hits the media there will be a storm." She smiled "you don't have to worry I will deal with the outcry."

Eric sat quietly then said, "I'm not sure why Doctor Sanford didn't speak with the board prior to the meeting? I assumed he had briefed them. They were shocked by my presentation. He is going to have a hard time with the board. I hope he doesn't lose his position."

Shirley looked directly at Eric, "I'm sure he plans on resigning."

"No," Eric said sitting up. "He is a great administrator. The students and faculty trust him and like him. Why would he resign?"

Shirley smiled slightly. "He has been eligible to retire for many cycles. As great an administrator as he is, he no doubt wants to step down and slow down. There are other things he may want to do." She stopped talking, allowing Eric to consider what she said. After a short while she continued. "He has probably spoken to Doctor Ringling about resigning. That is why he was so bold and spoke out when Brenda Norwich was so argumentative with him, as is usual. He challenged her because she is not going to be able to harm him. It is no secret she wants him gone and to have Burrell replace him. Doctor Sanford has made sure that won't happen by embarrassing her. Burrell will no doubt be replaced for leaking information to Brenda."

"I hadn't thought of that, but it makes sense. Do you think Burrell will be terminated?"

Shirley walked to Eric placing her hands on his face. "You need to examine the project and not worry honey." She kissed him lightly on the lips and walked away.

That evening as Eric and Shirley watched the evening broadcast the lead story was about the board meeting. The handsome man behind a large desk, smiled into the camera. "Well the routine Education Board of Directors Meeting was certainly anything but routine. Doctor Eric Franklin reported a student's carousel from sixty lunar cycles was still running. In addition to that remarkable statement, there appears to be tiny people inside who have a complex society. We have an expert who can give us more information on this amazing development."

He turned to another man sitting at the long table. "Doctor Evan Ellis, what do you think of these developments, reported by Doctor Franklin?"

The man smiled, "it's of course ridiculous there is no way what this man reported can be true." He laughed. "Any primary school student would realize it is a hoax. I mean really if the Doctor wants attention he needs to at least come up with something that is not so stupid! The man is a fake who wants attention. I can't believe the University would allow him to make such a presentation."

Allen Rushing, the lead journalist asked, "have you seen any of the information? I have looked at Doctor Franklin's presentation the University presented. I am not a scientist, with Doctor Franklin's credentials, but it does look compelling."

Doctor Ellis laughed, "compelling, are you serious? I find it hard to believe a journalist with your reputation would even give this obvious hoax any credibility! I looked at the presentation and it is flawed."

The interview ended. Shirley was on her small hand held computer. Eric's brow furrowed, "my data is not flawed. Whoever this Doctor is, obviously has not studied the information."

Shirley, looking at her computer in her hand, nodded, "don't worry about it honey."

# Chapter IX

THE PEOPLE INSIDE THE carousel referred to the satellite as a moon, their planet they called Earth. Roger had made the decision to place a small camera on the Earth's moon so people could see for themselves what was happening inside the carousel. The signal was broadcast across Praque, and other planets in the galaxy. He also allowed access to the computer so people could read about the humanoid people's past and each cultures beliefs. Individuales could use their computer to see different parts of the planet. Each language was translated by artificial intelligence. The computer's firewall would not allow anyone to access it to make changes.

People were fascinated with the small inhabitants as they would go through their daily lives. Throughout the galaxy people anxiously gathered Information concerning the beliefs concerning different cultures on the Earth that was made available through the computer. The religious beliefs, government, and social values were read by anyone who was interested. The history of the Earth and the people from the present and past were read and studied with fascination. Most throughout the galaxy were intrigued by the entertainment of the small humanoid people. The music was downloaded which had to be translated. Many young men and women began to copy the odd style of dancing. The movies were also made available to the different planets.

It became a trend for people to begin to dress like many of the people on Earth. This did cause a controversy as many opposed the new fad.

Brenda Norwich made it clear Doctor Sanford had lost his mind. He had allowed the carousel to be viewed by anyone when it first of all should have been the board's decision to release the information. She said angrily. "This type of information should be studied by experts to determine if it is a hoax. It has not been established if Doctor Franklin has faked it. Information should be given in stages so people can understand what they are seeing and hearing. It is irresponsible for Doctor Sanford to release the information without any context."

There were many in the Government who agreed with Brenda. They were angry for not being briefed on the situation. Representative Jordan Gyminy who was chairman of the Ethics and Finance committee made it clear he was not pleased with being left out of information being presented before prior release.

"Northwestern University of Praque releasing this information before briefing my committee has shown not only irresponsibility but disrespect for the people who are in charge of the government. My committee should have been briefed prior to releasing the information. There will be a hearing, I promise you that and I will hold those responsible for this leak of information. I have no doubt this is a hoax, and I will prove it. Those responsible for this hoax will be incarcerated."

Information concerning the carousel caused a sensation with the entire galaxy. People began to post their thoughts and strong opinions. Misinformation began to spread throughout the computer information system that linked all computers. Many stated it was only artificial intelligence that had created virtual reality, a sophisticated hologram. The program was computer generated. Most believed it was real and challenged others to prove it wasn't. Hard feelings were felt as the conversations often became ugly. People began to take sides.

The religious views on Praque as well as other planets varied depending on the individual's beliefs. There was one religion on Praque which had spread throughout the galaxy. The religion had two different views of worshiping. The Shelet viewpoint was a strict adherence to the sacred word. Emerial Juddings was the Premier Reverend of the Shelet Religion. Omniprest, interpred the sacred word in a more liberal way. There were often disagreements in the interpretation of how religion should be viewed. The difference in worshiping had split people with each having strong views. Arguments often left people angry, and suspicious of those who they opposed.

Reverend Juddings sat in the studio with Allen Rushing. Allen smiled saying "we are honored to have as our guest Primer Reverend Emerial Juddings. Thank You for being here Reverend."

Emerial, wearing his white formal robes trimmed in scarlet red and gold, he wore his small hat that matched his robe. He smiled "It is a pleasure Allen, thank you for allowing me a humble servant of the Lord to be here."

"Tell me Reverend, what are your thoughts on this carousel that has been running for sixty lunar cycles? How does the church view this issue?"

Reverend Juddings dropped his smile. "It is an abomination. I and most of the world do not believe this is real. It is obviously a hoax. It needs to be shut down immediately."

"Why shut it down Reverend?" Allan asked.

"Because it is blasphemy, an abomination that insults the Lord. Life cannot simply begin! We all know the Lord breathed out and life was created. Is Doctor Franklin God, I would say not. If this is not some kind of hologram, then he has manipulated and somehow created these beings. Which is unethical and I demand this project be terminated immediately!"

"Reverend with respect, the people on the carousel have a religion, one God as we do. They believe in heaven as we do, in addition believe they have a soul as we do. Shouldn't they have rights as we do?'

"No!" Reverend Juddings shouted. "These beings were created in a lab, not by the Lord! You are being blasphemous by insulting the Lord!"

"I do not believe I am showing blasphemy, or disrespecting the Lord. I am asking a question I believe is fair." Allen said, obviously irritated.

"It is obvious to all viewers, you are allowing your personal beliefs to cloud your judgment. You no doubt by your lack of respect are of a religion that is ignorant of how the sacred word is to be read. The project will be terminated!" Reverend Juddings said, sneering at Allen.

"You insulting the Omniprest religion is insulting, Reverend."

Reverend Juddings sighed. "I was told if I came on the air with you, I would be insulted, but I thought, foolishly I see, it was a mistake."

He stood up and walked off the set.

Eric, watching with Shirley, said "That didn't go so well."

"Oh, no honey, that went exactly as Reverend Juddings intended. He is playing the victim, with his false humility." She held Eric's hand "that's why I love you Eric. You believe there is good in people."

"Don't you?" he asked surprised.

"Yes, but I don't see it in the courtroom."

# Chapter X

LATE IN THE AFTERNOON Eric returned home. Shirley was in the den looking into the screen of her monitor. She turned to see Eric walk in, "hey Eric how was your day honey?"

Eric frowned as he sat down. "I was notified by Doctor Sanford Premier Reverend Juddings has filed a suit demanding the carousel project be shut down."

"I know I spoke with Doctor Sanford. I will be representing the University. Chief Judge Wilkins has approved my leave as a judge." Shirley said smiling.

"I'm concerned the project will be shut down. There is so much to learn. Scientists from across the galaxy are studying the project." Eric was not smiling.

"I've been preparing the case for some time. I don't believe the project will be shut down. I'm confident even if Judge Seyfierd, who will most likely be the judge, is selected. He is a devout Shelet, and has always been sympathetic to the church. He will have to go with the evidence." Shirley said, trying to reassure Eric.

"So how are things at the University with the new year?" Shirley asked pleasantly

Eric continued to frown. "Most students believe the carousel is what it is, an anomaly. Some of the more radical, and outspoken are insisting it is a hoax. I have given lectures but they continue to ignore the facts and keep quoting the fake information being put out by the extremist. They are truly ignorant."

"They have a right to their opinion," Shirley said quietly.

"Yes everybody has a right to be stupid if they choose not to accept facts." Eric sat up, "I truly don't understand how people who are presented with facts can simply ignore them, and believe what they want. Even if it is proven wrong, people ignore facts. It is stupid."

Shirley walked to Eric taking his hand helping him stand up. She hugged him tightly, then kissed him. She stared into his eyes. "Prepare yourself Doctor, You haven't seen anything yet. It is about to get a whole lot more stupid."

Eric sat next to Doctor Sanford and Betsy in the courtroom a week later. Shirley sat at a small desk across from Michael Parsons who represented the Church.

Judge Seyfierd walked in, sitting behind a large table. He was an older man who was overweight and balding. He looked over papers in front of him. He looked up, "Are we prepared?"

"Yes," both attorney's answered.

"All right then, before us is a suit that asks this court to shut down a project Northwestern University of Praque currently has that is operational. I believe it has been running for sixty lunar cycles. Northwestern University objects wanting to study the project." He looked up "are there any additions to the original suit, if not we will begin."

Michael stood up "thank you Judge Seyfierd, The Church contends this project is an abomination to society and is blasphemes to what the church stands for. This project is not for the good of society. This project needs to be terminated before more problems are caused to not only this planet but others in the galaxy. There are numerous reports of violence that has occured because of the tension this project has caused. Our people are becoming obsessed with this project. It is an experiment that is no doubt a hoax, if not then the physics and science rules will need to be rewritten. The Church contends this program, and that is what it is a project, is causing disturbances across the galaxy. I have for the court, letters of support from the Master Chief of Law Enforcement, and many congressmen. I do apologize to you Judge Seyfierd, this is a waste of your time and the court system. Northwestern University needs to shut down this project before it becomes more dangerous for society." Michael sat down.

Shirley stood up "Northwestern University disagrees." She sat down.

Eric stared at Shirley's back. "That's it?" he thought, "the other side gives a grand speech and Shirley says "Northwestern University disagrees." He looked past Doctor Sanford hearing Betsy giggling.

Michael looked at Shirley curiously, then stood up "I ask Premier Reverend Emerial Juddings to take the stand."

Reverend Juddings rose slowly from the front of the audience and walked slowly and deliberately to the stand. His white robes flowing as he approached the stand. He turned and looked solemnly at the Judge. "I ask your testimony to be honest, will you abide by this?" Judge Seyfierd asked, solemnly.

"I swear I will." Reverend Juddings said loudly and solemnly. He sat down arranging his robes.

Michael sitting asked, "Reverend why did you bring this suit against the University?"

"I believe the sacred word that has been inspired by our Lord should always be honored. It is to my shock and displeasure to see Northwestern University lower itself to such degradation as to allow this abomination to continue." Reverend Juddings said frowning.

"Reverend, can you explain the degradation you believe has happened?"

He sighed, sneering, "This abomination has been created by the hand of man, not by our Lord. That is the only explanation. I know there have been scientists that have said they cannot see where the beings on the planet were created. It was not the Lord, so they were created by man, or somehow mutated."

The Reverend would expound for two hours quoting from scriptures. He was in his element. The cameras were on as he was the center of attention. He knew how to speak and was confident as he explained his point of view.

When the Reverend finished speaking Michael looked at the Judge, "I have nothing else Judge."

Shirley looked directly at Reverend Juddings, "prove it."

Reverend Juddings looked at her "prove what?" he looked confused as he smiled.

Shirley's stare was intense, "the sacred word?"

Reverend Juddings was shocked, "How dare you ask such a question. It is blasphemes!"

"No, it is not, Reverend. This is a court of law. You must prove all statements. You have quoted the scripture, accusing Northwestern University of not following the Lord's commandments. So prove the scriptures."

The Reverend sat quiet, he was shocked at being asked to prove the scriptures. Shirley sat quietly looking at Reverend Juddings. The tension in the room began to grow as the Reverend stared at Shirley, his anger growing.

Judge Seyfried finally said "perhaps you could restate your question Mrs. Franklin."

"Sure, Reverend, when was the sacred word first written? Please provide the exact date."

Reverend Juddings laughed. "The word was inspired by God, our Lord eons ago."

"Who wrote it? The men who were inspired?" Shirley asked, raising her voice.

"I nor anybody knows their names! This is ridiculous."

"Prove the Lord breathed out and life was created." Shirley asked her voice level.

"That is blasphemy!" He stood up pointing at Shirley "I will not sit here while this woman treats the sacred word with such disrespect!"

"You need to sit down Reverend!" The Judge said forcefully.

The Reverend stared at Judge Seyfried, "Are you going to allow this blasphemy in your court, Marty? You are a man of the word, how can you allow this kind of talk?"

Judge Seyfried's face was blue. "You need to sit down Reverend. Mrs. Franklin has the right to ask questions."

Reverend Juddings was shocked as he sat down looking at Michael.

Shirley said "Reverend, isn't it true the sacred word is based on faith. Believers in the word put their trust in its message because of faith?"

"Yes," he said glaring at Shirley.

"Okay, then, you have stated that the University is wrong with the project because of the sacred word. However, you are unable to prove the sacred word as this court demands. You ask us to have faith. I'm sorry Reverend, in this court, you are required to provide proof. So please prove the sacred word."

Reverend Juddings sat glaring at Shirley. Finally Shirley said "I will take it by your silence you cannot prove the sacred word." She looked at the Judge and said pleasantly. "I have nothing further with the Reverend."

Reverend Juddings stood up slowly staring at Shirley. He walked back to his seat in the front and sat down. Judge Seyfried was visibly shaken. He looked at Michael who sat quiet. "You may proceed."

"Anne Hamilton, please take the stand."

Anne, wearing a simple blue dress, walked to the front and sat in the old worn chair looking at Michael.

"So how did you rig the carousel to run for sixty lunar cycles?" Michael's tone was sarcastic.

Anne smiled pleasantly. "Would the gentleman please repeat the question, and be more professional." She turned looking at the Judge. "I find this man rude and unprofessional. Would you instruct the gentleman to be more respectful. If not in your court, at the least to an Elder."

The Judge was surprised. Witness did not address him. "Answer the question Elder!" Michael repeated.

Anne turned, "I suppose manors are no longer used in a court setting. I followed all the parameters set out by my instructor, Elder Fogheart."

"What were those parameters?" Michael asked more politely.

"The same parameters all students were required at that time. I don't remember the exact protocols used. Perhaps you could explain the parameters of the carousel project when you were in your second year, it may help me remember."

Michael's face turned blue. "I do not appreciate your tone Elder Hamilton!"

Anne looked directly at Michael. "I do not remember the exact parameters, no more than you do. Yet you attack me for not being able to respond.

Michael was now angry. "Why is it Elder Hamilton your carousel is still running?

"I don't know."

"You were not a good student. Isn't that correct!" Michael asked, raising his voice.

"Define a good student?" Anne asked calmly."

"Answer the question!" Michael yelled.

Judge Seyfierd frowned. "That is enough, I will not have you yelling in this court. Do you understand sir?"

Michael gained his composure. He realized Anne Hamilton was not intimidated in the courtroom.

"How did you do in School Elder Hamilton?" He asked calmly.

"I was average. Science and Math were difficult. I passed and I was above average in all other subjects." Anne remained calm looking at Michael.

"Was there anything unusual about your carousel?

"Yes, it continued to run when the school lunar cycle ended."

Shirley smiled slightly. She glanced at Michael who was visibly upset.

Michael sat quiet for a while then asked. "The carousel was still running, so why didn't Elder Fogheart turn it off?"

"I cannot speak for Elder Fogheart. He simply said "the carousel will stop in a few days." He placed it in a box. Bobby Horton, who was a fellow student and I took all of the projects and placed them in a closet in the basement." She leaned forward, her stare intense. "That is all I know sir."

"No further questions." Michael said glaring.

Shirley smiled pleasantly. "I have no questions for Elder Hamilton."

Anne stepped down walking back to her seat in the audience.

# Chapter XI

ON THE SECOND DAY OF the hearing Eric was called to the stand. He was asked several questions by Michael. He answered all the questions, staying on the stand for two hours. Shirley did not ask any questions. Other scientists were called to the stand. Their answers were similar to Eric's. None of them could explain how the old carousel could be running after six solar cycles. The scientists were all baffled how humanoid creatures could be in the project, or how they were introduced into the project, or explain the complex society. Shirley did not ask any questions.

The hearing concluded the following day. Michael stood up and sighed. "Judge it is obvious from the testimony given, this project is an enigma. It should be shut down since it is causing so much controversy across our planet as well as other planets. As Premier Reverend Juddings has stated it is an abomination. Allow it to end before it causes more problems." He sat down.

Shirley stood up slowly, she smiled at the Judge knowing the camera was behind him. She looked professional in her conservative dress that went to her knees, her hair and makeup was perfect. Shirley made sure she was directly in front of the camera.

"Judge Seyfeired, I do not question Premier Reverend Juddings, or his views. I am a believer in the sacred word. But our rule of laws requires facts. Our religion is based on faith. No evidence has been presented to justify shutting down this project that is an enigma as my colleague has stated. We as a society have an opportunity to learn from this new world. Allow academics of all levels to study it and learn from this enigma that may be a gift from the Lord." She sat down.

The court was in recess as the Judge walked out to consider the information presented. When he returned an hour later the audience sat in anticipation.

Judge Seyfierd looked sternly saying, "I have considered all evidence provided. This carousel project is a mystery. I do not find any reason the project should be shut down." He stood up and walked out.

Michael smiled at Shirley. "I knew it was a long shot but I do represent the church."

Shirley smiled. "You put on a good case, but I doubt this is over. Judge Seyfierd had little choice. I'm sure Reverend Juddings will not take this well."

That evening Shirley sat in Doctor Sanford's house with Eric. Betsy made sure Eric and Shirley were comfortable before she sat down. Roger smiled broadly, "you did a great job Shirley. Perhaps we can put this all behind us and study this anomaly."

"I doubt this is over. The court was only the opening shot. It is going to get ugly, I'm hearing conservative Representatives have opened an investigation. They don't have to follow the strict rules of the court. I suspect we will be at the capitol soon."

Roger leaned back, "I've been hearing the same thing. Representatives love being in front of the camera. I am concerned that protests are getting larger."

As it grew late Eric stood up taking Shirley's hand, "we should go. Thank you for the evening."

Betsy followed them to the door. "Oh, by the way Judge Franklin, I recently received a citation which I believe was unjust. Could we talk about it sometime?"

Shirley giggled, Roger let out his breath, "Betsy we talked about this. It is not appropriate to ask Shirley to intervene in a personal matter."

"Just look into it Shirley, you will see I'm right."

It was a nice cool evening. Eric held Shiley's hand as they walked home. "You did a good job Shirley. I was concerned for a while when you didn't ask any questions other than Reverend Juddings."

Shirley smiled as they continued to walk home.

# Chapter XII

REVEREND EMERIAL JUDDINGS sat in a large overstuffed chair in his study. He stared at the drink in his hand as the anger grew inside him. "I can not believe Marty Seyfierd, who is a staunch believer attending my church, would allow this abomination to continue!"

Michael sat quiet, then said in a low voice, "He didn't have a choice. He is constrained by the law. I told you that our case was not strong. It is our responsibility to prove the facts. They just were not there!"

The sacred word is our facts! The Lord is on our side, that should be enough!" The Reverend shouted, his face turning blue with rage.

"I understand your disappointment, Reverend, but the court has strict rules to follow." Michael said firmly."

"Well that is just stupid." Brenda said, taking a drink and sitting the glass on a small table. "This project is an abomination, little men created inside an old carousel is wrong. Roger Sanford and Eric Franklin need to be locked up." She stared angrily at Michael. "Not only that he has demoted Burrell, my son in law who should be the Chancellor! What do you plan on doing about that Michael? You are making a good salary, earn it!"

"It is an internal matter. Burrell allowed himself to be set up by Doctor Sanford. It is his decision, and he has the authority to hire, terminate, promote, and demote how he choses." Michael said calmly.

Brenda stared angrily at Michael. I'll speak to friends in the government, if you can not handle this Michael."

"How are we going to shut this shameful project down Michael? I mean this is blasmous, we can not allow it to continue! Emerial yelled.

Michael sighed. "The project can not be shut down legally. I realize you are angry, but we lost in court. You're not suggesting we break the law?"

Brenda leaned forward, "we'll see how the University handles a hearing with government Representatives who are true believers. The rules are different." Brenda said smugly.

Michael looked directly at her. "Shirley Franklin is a great attorney. I wonder how the Representatives will handle her?"

"I have spoken with William Jackson, the Master Chief Law Enforcement of Phram. He will help." Emerial said smiling.

THE FOLLOWING AFTERNOON Eric stopped as he approached the University. A large crowd of men and women were on the lawn protesting. Many were holding signs that read Abomination, Blasphemous, and other slogans. The crowd began yelling at Eric as he approached the steps to his building. The angry words and insults surprised him. He continued into his building heading for his office.

Inside his office Sally, an undergraduate assistant, met him at the door; her eyes were wide. "You have messages on the computer. They are not nice, some are threatening. Doctor Sanford has contacted Law Enforcement."

Eric was shocked at the messages. Most were threatening, as others accused him of being a fraud, and not a true believer of the sacred word."

It would be a long day. Eric had to deal with students questioning his ethics as other students defended him in class. He tried to keep the class on track, but many students only wanted to argue. Other instructors experienced the same issues in their classes. Many outspoken students disrupted classes making it difficult for instructors. Students became angry at the disruption from the radicals who continued to argue.

The large crowd did not disburse but grew in numbers. Some students joined the protesters. Eric found it difficult to walk past the crowd as they yelled at him.

When he arrived at home he explained the protesters and their disruption of the University. Shirley sat listening intently. She sighed, "It's not going to get any better. A summons arrived today, you are to appear before a hearing with Representatives next week. They are investigating your enigma." She smiled sweetly, "don't worry honey, you have a great attorney."

REPRESENTATIVE JORDAN Gymini was anxious for the hearing to begin. He had been speaking to Journalists for weeks about the carousel project. He made it clear it was a hoax and he would shut it down. His committee would get the truth and the galaxy would see how ridiculous this whole thing was. He blasted the court system for not doing its job and shutting down the project when it had the information in front of them. He spoke of how weak the court system had become with too many liberal judges tolerating the law not being followed as it was intended. He promised to correct that mistake.

He felt confident knowing the majority of his committee agreed with him. They were all staunch Shelet members. The few who were Omniprest would be voted down. They were soft and tolerant of those who believed differently. Ron Norton, the presiding Emier, leader of the current Government, who had recently been elected would support him.

Jordan felt confident knowing he would make this Doctor Franklin look like a fool. Michael Parsons had briefed him on the particular issues. Michael had warned him, being concerned that Eric's wife Shirley was a good attorney. He was not worried. He had been chairman for a long time and he always won. Jordan knew Eric and Shirley would have to walk past the protesters who were gathered in front of the Capitol. He was certain they would intimidate them. Which was his hope.

Primer Reverend Juddings had testified before the hearing that morning. He was eloquent in quoting the sacred scripture. The protesters cheered when he walked by them on his way to the hearing. Everything was going as he had planned. With the monitors on everyone in the galaxy would see him as the hearing was broadcasted. That excited him. Also Reverend Juddings would be pleased with him. That was an added bonus.

Eric sat down at the table in front of the panel of Representatives that afternoon. There were seven total. Shirley was sitting next to him.

Representative Gymini wasted no time. He attacked Eric immediately.

"Doctor Franklin, please explain to this committee how a carousel can run sixty lunar cycles?"

"I can't."

"You mean you won't?"

"No, I do not know how it has continued to operate for sixty lunar cycles."

"Ridiculous, you expect us to believe a carousel can actually run that long!"

"I have provided information to the committee concerning this project."

"You lied on this information!" Representative Gymni sneered.

Shirley leaned forward, "prove it."

Jordan looked at the beautiful woman staring intently at him. "It is a lie, Doctor Franklin faked the data."

"Then you can prove it. Twenty Two scientists signed off on the information. Are you saying they all lied?"

Jordan shook his head and laughed. "Sixty lunar cycles? An ancient archaic carousel can run that long! Are you serious?"

"I said prove your slanderous statement sir!" Shirley was on her feet, her hands flat on the table. Raising her voice with intensity She stared hard at Jordan. "You prove your statement, Doctor Franklin lied, along with twenty two scientists, or withdraw the question!"

The rage was building inside Jordan. He was not used to anyone speaking so harshly to him. He was not to be challenged. He, however, was a politician. He smiled "I have misspoke. I withdraw the statement." he looked at Eric, seeing Shirley sit down looking calmly at him.

"Doctor Franklin, How did the little creatures you call humanoid come into existence?"

"I don't know."

"Expand on your answer, Doctor!" Jordan yelled.

Shirley said, "Question has been answered Representative Gymini."

"I want an answer, not this lame weak response." Jordan's face showed rage.

"Question was answered." Shirley said calmly.

Jordan was obviously angry, "I would like to ask a question Chairman Gymini." Jordan looked to see Janice Anderson looking at him. "Denied."

"I have a right to ask a question. The committee rules state all members are afforded an opportunity to speak. Would you like to see the rules, I have a copy here."

Jordan waved his hand dismissively. "Ask then."

Janice smiled "Doctor Franklin in the information provided, you as well as other scientists do not provide information concerning how the humanoid people came into existence in the carousel. Will you explain why?"

"The carousel has a computer that records all information that occurs. Including new species, or species that go extinct. Nowhere is there information about the humanoid people. None of the scientists that have investigated this project has been able to find that information. They appear but we do not know how. I do not know."

"You call them people? Really, how do you determine that? They are creatures created like a tree or animal." Jordan laughed.

"Trees, and animals do not create complex societies, with education systems, religious, and monetary systems. They have cultures, technology, families and believe they have a soul and when they die will go to heaven."

"What if they don't go to heaven?" Jordan asked sarcastically.

Shirley leaned forward, "then you can ask them when you arrive at your final destination."

People in the audience laughed, as well as those on the committee. Jordan's face was blue with rage. He stared at Shirley who sat back calmly looking back at him.

Jordan gained his composure, "There are experts who disagree with your analysis and results. They say you are a fraud, Doctor Franklin."

Shirley sat up, "Are you referring to Doctor Evan Ellis?" Shirley smiled. "That man loves being interviewed. You do know Representative Gymini, Doctor Ellis is a former secondary school literature instructor. He is a science fiction writer." Shirley began to laugh. "Are you saying a science fiction writer is your expert?" Shirley sat back laughing.

Eric watched Shirley then said "I do not know Doctor Ellis, and am not aware of him inspecting the carousel."

More questions were asked by the panel. The majority were hostile. Each time Shirley countered the hostility. The committee was becoming frustrated as it was obvious they were losing control of the hearing. This was upsetting to Jordan who was always in control. Finally as the hearing durg on Shirley said loudly, "the questions being asked are being repeated. It is obvious there is nothing further. This is a waste of time."

"You don't decide that, I decide when the hearing is over." Jordan said in a controlled voice.

"This is ridiculous, and a waste of time." She sat back waving her hand, "Alrighty then please continue!" Shirley said loudly, obviously angry.

"Doctor Franklin explain how an antiquated generator that is not even made anymore can run for six solar cycles." Jordan asked.

Eric leaned back looking at Shirley, whispering. "I can take this guy. He is a few years older and heavier, but I can take him."

"I thank you could too, but it would be unprofessional seeing him on the air getting his butt kicked. Don't do it."

Shirley sat up speaking loudly looking at Jordan "I have informed my client not to answer the question since it is so incredibly stupid."

Jordan's face was deep blue. The rage was apparent. "You will answer the question! Now!"

"No he will not!" Shirley said pleasantly.

Jordan could see people trying not to laugh. He was infuriated. "You are a Doctor, can't you explain the workings of a generator?"

"Yes, it is rather a simple device that is powered by an outside source. In this case by light. That would be solar. Since the carousel was in a box, in a basement closet, it cannot possibly have had power. I do not know."

After three hours the hearing ended. Eric and Shirley walked out. On the trolly Eric looked at Shirley. "I never realized how scarry you are. I now know why you always win an argument."

Shirley smiled, "Don't make me mad honey."

# Chapter XIII

THE FOLLOWING MORNING the committee met considering the vote to shut down the project. Jordan spoke at length of the situation and how it was obvious there was more than enough evidence to shut the project down. He allowed others to speak with the exception of the Omniprest. When Janice Anderson objected, holding up the rules, She was allowed a few minutes to speak. Janice questioned how there was a hearing that did not provide any evidence. There was a great sermon that did not provide any evidence as to why this scientific project should be shut down. She was cut off in the middle of her talk. The measure passed with all Shelet members voting yes. The measure would be sent to the Emier and with his signature it would be law. He had won.

Jordan was in his office when his assistant walked into the room. His eyes were wide. "Sir, Emier Norton has denied your measure."

Jordan was shocked. "That's not right. Ron is a friend we go way back. He is a staunch believer, and attends Reverend Juddings church."

The young man handed a paper to Jordan. He looked at it in disbelief. He could not believe what he was seeing, the Emier had denied the measure.

He was on his feet walking quickly out of his office. He rode the escalator to the top floor and walked immediately into the Emiers office. He walked past the secretary's desk and opened the door, throwing it open. "Why did you deny my measure!"

Ron stood up with anger apparent on his face. "People are seen in this office when I allow them in. You have not been invited Jordan."

Jordan was surprised. "You denied my measure, I want an answer why."

"You don't make demands of me in my office, and I don't have to give you an explanation Representative Gymani!" Ron yelled.

Jordan stepped back. "Ron, you and I have been together for a long time. What is going on?"

"Your committee hearing was a joke. Mrs. Franklin made you and the rest of your radical minions look ridiculous. Have you been paying attention to what the journalists are saying? Are you even aware of how the general public feels about this carousel enigma?"

Jordan stood mute. When he found his voice said, "I don't pay attention to those clowns. They are only good for when I need them. I have the population on my side."

"No, Jordan you do not. The majority of people on Praque, and other planets support this carousel project. You and Reverend Juddings and the few elite are out of touch. I am not against the project. I find it fascinating, it has tremendous public support, In addition to scientific study. You however, are too busy kissing The Reverends, holy backside to understand. Now get out of my office before I have security drag you out. I would do it myself but I'm Emier, that would be unprofessional."

Jordan walked out stunned.

# Chapter XIV

RITA NORTON OPENED the door seeing Reverend Juddings standing on the porch. He was wearing his casual Robe that was black trimmed in silver. His small hat matched his robe.

Rita smiled warmly, "Reverend please come in."

Reverend Juddings did not smile as he stepped inside the house. He followed Rita to a large open room. "Ron, Reverend Juddings is here."

Ron stood up sitting the small hand held computer on a table. He smiled "It's good to have you in my home Reverend. I've been expecting you."

Rita sat down in a chair next to Ron. Reverend Juddings did not smile as he sat down; he stared at Ron. "Why in the name of the most high Lord would you deny a measure Representative Jordan Gymni offered you? That does not make sense since you are a good Shelet member. I expected you to approve the measure and shut down this abomination!"

Ron leaned forward, "It was not your choice Reverend, it was mine." He felt Rita's hand on his. He glanced at her, seeing the look in her eye. He needed to proceed carefully. "I do not answer to you. You will not instruct me on how to do the work I was elected to do by the people of this country."

"I expect you to follow the commands of the sacred word!" Reverend Juddings yelled.

Ron stood up slowly, "You are not the Lord himself. You will not treat me as if I am a small child to be bullied. I do not work for you or the church."

"Ron sit down." Rita said softly.

Ron sat down as he and Emerial stared at each other. Emerial took a deep breath,

"I expect you to do what is right. This carousel project is an abomination."

"I don't think so. Most people disagree with you and the elite."

Reverend Juddings face was blue with rage. "It is an abomination, because I say it is!"

The three sat silently when Rita stood up. "Reverend, Ron and I have decided to attend the Onniprest church. I believe it is time for you to leave my home."

The Reverend sat stunned. No one left his church, and he was being dismissed. His church was the largest on the planet as well as any other planet in the galaxy. He slowly stood up. "You are leaving my church? Am I to understand you are dismissing me? I'm the Premiere Reverend!"

"Yes we are." Rita said, staring at him. "I do not believe Ron or I need to give you an explanation. Please leave my home."

Reverend Juddings rose slowly staring hard at Ron and Rita. "You will regret this," he said growling.

Ron stepped close to him. "Be careful who you threaten Emerial."

Reverend Juddings turned and walked out of the house slamming the door behind him.

Emerial Juddings sat in an overstuffed chair in his office, anger growing inside him. He looked at the group of people who had gathered in his office. He glared at the men and women, "I can't believe Ron has abandoned us. The Emier, who I had placed great hope in to help promote my cause. I just can't believe he has betrayed me."

"What we need is a long drawn out investigation. Representative Gymni needs to investigate Emier Norton for a sexual scandal, or misappropriation of finances." Brenda stated smugly.

"Is there a problem with the government's finances? Has the Emier been involved in a sexual scandal? I'm not aware of any of these accusations." Michael said, sitting up in his chair.

Brenda laughed, "we just need to accuse the man, who cares if it is true?" She laughed, saying "Journalists love a good scandal. The more he defends himself the more guilty he appears."

Michael stared in disbelief. "You want to create a scandal that is a lie. The issue with that is Emier Norton will no doubt have Shirley Franklin as his attorney. She handled Representative Gymni and his goon squad very well."

Master Chief Jackson frowned, "that woman is a nuisance. Perhaps she will be in an accident."

"You want to kill her? You're talking about murder Master Chief." Michael said, stunned.

"No one said murder, accidents do happen!" Jackson screamed.

"I'm aware of that Chief!" Michael yelled back. "The old days of taking out rivals you and Brenda have done, are wrong!" Michael stood up. He was so angry his face was a deep blue. He turned looking at Emerial, "Are you okay with this Reverend? Killing a rival, smearing a good man's name because he doesn't do exactly as you ask? Where in the sacred word does it say, "You may take the life of a rival if you are offended!"

Emerial was on his feet, "how dare you speak to me this way Michael! I am the Premier Reverend! I am the most powerful man in this galaxy. The Lord has blessed me and I will carry out his word!"

"You need to find another lawyer, Premier Reverend. I will not be a part of this plot to kill, or lie. How do you justify that Reverend?" Michael had lowered his voice as he stared at Emerial.

The two men glared at each other. Emerial took a breath allowing it to slowly escape. "I do not and will not condone murder, or slander."

Master Chief Jackson stood up, "No one has said we will murder anyone. I simply said sometimes accidents happen. I have no intention of causing an accident."

"No, you will hire a thug to do your dirty work." Michael said glaring back at Jackson.

"Michael, William is not suggesting anything illegal. He is just speaking out in frustration. You need to settle down. You are the church's attorney. It is your obligation to defend it." Emerial said in a calm voice.

Michael shook his head, "No, you need to get another attorney, I will submit my resignation in the morning." Michael said as he walked out of the room.

Emerel sat down. "I will speak with him in the morning when he settles down. I want no more talk of accidents or government hearings in this office." He sat silently for a while, then said as he smiled slyly, "You need to go out and do what you can to protect the church and myself." He smiled as he picked up his glass.

# Chapter XV

SHIRLEY WAS SURPRISED when she walked into her office seeing Eric sitting in a chair looking at his hand held computer. He looked up smiling. "Hey, how's the most beautiful Judge in the galaxy doing?"

Shirley smiled. "Well it has been a rough week." She sat down behind her desk as she frowned. "Journalist in my courtroom every day asking about the carousel project. It is getting tiresome. They are looking for the sensational, not one of them seems interested in facts. I suppose facts are too boring. So you just happened to be in the neighborhood and stopped by?"

Eric smiled "I was missing you. I thought I would take you out for a nice dinner."

"The large crowd that is growing outside the courthouse has anything to do with you meeting me here?" Shirley said, dropping her smile.

Eric sat up straight and leaned forward, "I'm worried this protest is getting out of hand. Reverend Juddings has been on the broadcast monitor talking about the great abomination. He is encouraging them to fight against this abomination. Saying crazy things like "if you don't fight for your religion, you won't have a religion." The man is becoming hysterical ranting and raving about how the courts have let us all down. The Lord is angry and those who are true believers should act. His supporters are not rational. I want to make sure you're safe."

Shirley stood up picking up her purse. "I am hungry, let's go."

When they stepped out of the door onto the porch of the courthouse, Eric could see the crowd had grown. He saw in the back a line of Law Enforcement Officers. He took a deep breath, took Shirley's hand and walked slowly down the steps. He could see the trolly coming. He thought they just needed to walk past the large crowd and get to the trolly.

The crowd became excited seeing Eric and Shirley. The people began yelling at the couple as they walked down the steps. The crowd surged forward as Eric turned walking toward the street. Soon they were surrounded by the crowd. Eric pulled Shirley behind him and tried to push his way through. The crowd became enraged and pushed back.

Eric felt a sharp pain on the side of his head as someone had punched him. Holding Shirley's hand tight he pushed hard trying to get out of the crowd. The crowd was in a frenzy as people began hitting Eric. There was no way out as the mob attacked.

Eric turned grabbing Shirley holding her close attempting to shield her from the blows of the crowd. They both fell as Eric covered her. The kicks and punches became more violent.

A young officer in the police line seeing the beating stepped forward. The Commander in charge yelled "back in line we are not to engage the protesters!"

The young officer hesitated hearing an order from his superior officer. He watched helplessly as the crowd became more violent. He looked at the Commander who was smiling watching the crowd beat two civilians. He closed his eyes then opened them, pulled his large electronic stick and charged the crowd. He heard the Commander screaming, "get back in line! We are not to engage the protesters!"

The young officer began fighting his way through the crowd. The crowd was surprised, then turned on the young officer. Officers who had formed the line began running to his defense. The Commander ran at them screaming for them to get back in line. The officers refused and continued to fight the crowd.

More officers left the line attacking the crowd. Soon armed officers with electronic sticks had control of the crowd as many in the mob turned and ran. The powerful electronic sticks stunned men and women in the crowd knocking them down. Ambulances were called as wounded officers and protesters were treated for injuries. Eric and Shirley, along with many officers and protesters were taken to a hospital.

That evening as the news was broadcast across the planet. People were shocked to see protesters attacking Eric and Shirley. They watched in horror as Law Enforcement stood by until an officer went to their defense. The Commander was shown screaming at the officer, and others as more officers attacked the crowd. Journalists were shocked by the scene. All of them condemned the Commander and Officers who stood by watching the mob attack.

The following day those officers who chose to disobey a direct order and engaged the protesters were terminated. Master Chief Jackson standing in front of the steps of the headquarters of Law Enforcement condemned the officers for attacking a peaceful protest. He insisted Eric and Shirley Franklin had insulted the crowd, but he did concede there were perhaps a few who were out of line by punching the Franklins who had started the riot.

That afternoon half the police force in Phram resigned. The following day more officers resigned.

Emier Ron Norton walked into the waiting room of the largest hospital in Phram. He saw a young woman holding a baby staring out a large window. She turned, seeing him walking toward her. She immediately stood up looking down, which was a sign of respect.

Ron reached out, taking her small face in his hands. He lifted her face looking directly at her. Tears fell from her eyes as she sobbed, "They fired Billy."

"I know Mrs. Myers, I promise you I will take care of that miscarage of justice. The Doctors say Billy will be alright. He will go home in a few days. You need to keep your faith."

She smiled at Ron.

Ron spoke with many of the families of the officers who had been hurt in the riot. He walked to a small room seeing Shirley sitting in a chair. She looked up seeing him walk into her room. She stood up as he took her in his arms holding her close. She cried on his shoulder. "I will take care of this, I promise Mrs. Franklin. What happened was wrong."

Shirley broke the embrace "Eric is on life support. I, I don't know if he will survive. He saved me."

"He will live. Have faith, don't give up on him or the Lord." Ron was visibly upset.

"The Doctors say you will be released today. I have a vehicle ready to take you home. Military officers will be outside your home. You will be safe."

"Thank you." Shirley said softly

"Also be aware Journalists are outside. I can have my officers escort you to the vehicle."

"Thank you Emier, but I want to speak to them. This way they can all see the results of a peaceful demonstration."

Ron frowned seeing the bruised swollen face of Shirley.

Shirley stepped outside the hospital as Journalists swarmed her. She stood silent allowing the cameras to get a view of her face. She said, "Master Chief Jackson says a peaceful protest occurred. Twenty seven officers in the hospital, my husband on life support. He lies, and expects people to believe him. And by the way, where is Premier Reverend Juddings? He has been very outspoken about how we need to fight for our faith, we need to fight for our Lord. He has demanded a holy war. Well he has received what he asked for. A violent mob who has fought for him. He should let us all know if he agrees with Master

Chief Jackson?" Shirley walked away with two large Military Officers beside her.

Ron had waited inside the hospital watching Shirley. When she finished he walked out of the hospital. Journalists swarmed him.

"I am sick from what I have seen. I have spoken to those brave officers who fought for justice, and their families. I am proud of them. Military will be on standby in the city to fill in for those officers who were wrongfully terminated. I ask those who resigned to please return. I will do everything I can to reverse the termination of those heroes who have been treated so wrong by a corrupt system." He laughed. "I will, even though the Elitist Representative Gymni is investigating me for lies. His smear campaign is intended to distract from this riot. I welcome his hearing in front of his arrogant members who are in the hands of the most elite."

Ron answered questions as he walked to his vehicle.

# Chapter XVI

MICHAEL PARSONS TOOK a deep breath, let it out slowly, opened the door and walked into Reverend Juddings office. Emerial stood up from his chair walking toward him. "Michael, I am so glad you are here. We have a problem needing attention."

Michael held up his hand, "I resigned Reverend, I am no longer the church's attorney."

"You're a member of the church, you can give us some guidance." Emerial pleaded.

Michael sat in a chair looking at Brenda Norwich and Master Chief Jackson. He looked at Reverend Juddings. "I have no advice for you Reverend. You listened to your old cronies. They of course do not realize the world has moved on from them and their old ways. Elder Norwich no longer has anyone left who will listen to her. All her powerful friends have retired and no longer have authority. Master Chief Jackson has outlived his time. The old ways of cracking heads and getting away with it no longer work. You, however, chose their council."

"I have friends in the government who listen to me. I will show you what elite people are capable of, Michael!" Brenda said, raising her voice.

"No you don't Brenda, you are an old elitist who people despise. No one in the government wants anything to do with you." Michael said, staring back at Brenda.

"What can we do Michael?" Emrial asked.

"Be honest, and humble. Journalists are beating you up nightly. The Church is under attack because of this riot. Your close association with Master Chief Jackson is a liability. He has lost control of his own force. Emier Norton has placed military in the city to enforce laws. Members of your congregation are leaving the church. You need to address this issue humbly. I mean no disrespect but your arrogance has condemned you."

"I am not arrogant, how dare you say such a thing about me!" Emerial said angrily.

"You asked for my opinion. Your words on the air have excited many to violence. Use the Journalist, to make this somewhat less about you and the church." Michael looked at Master Chief Jackson, "Someone needs to accept responsibility."

Jackson's face was blue. "I'm not taking the fall for this! We are all in on this!" He looked at the Reverend. "We are together on this Emerial."

"Perhaps you should consider the greater good. You should accept responsibility for, say, a poor choice. You are eligible for retirement. The church needs to not be blamed." Emerial said softly.

"You mean, cover your backside, not the church! You want me to be blamed for all the problems you created. I tried to help you Emerial!" Jackson yelled.

"Let's all calm down!" Brenda said, raising her voice. "We need to stay together! We blame the scientist, a poor decision on the Commander, we say the same thing enough times and people will believe it!" She sat quietly then said, "the general population is stupid. They will believe whatever they are told. We don't need proof, we continue to say the same thing over and over again and the public will be on our side. We use journalists who love controversy to spread our message. The more outrageous our words are, the more journalists will cover us. Radicals will spread misinformation and people will believe without verifying the report. ” She sat back smiling, “everyone loves a good conspiracy.”

Michael stood up and walked out of the room.

# Chapter XVII

CAPTAIN FIRST CLASS Terry Martin smiled brightly as two young women walked past him. "Good morning ladies."

They both smiled broadly at the nice looking officer. "Good morning Captain" they both said as they continued to walk past.

"Captain First Class," Terry thought to himself. "It's a common mistake," he thought. Most civilians did not understand the rank structure of the military. He had recently been promoted. Now his first duty was to patrol the streets of Pharm and be nice. His Superior officer had made it clear all military personnel were to be polite.

"Be nice, you hear me Captain's! You will ensure your personnel are polite! We do not need the general population thinking the military is taking over the Planet! There are enough crazies posting rumors and conspiracies about how we are staging a take over! Emier Norton has called on the military to keep the peace while the idiots in Law Enforcement figure out how to get their people back on the job! Now am I clear!"

"Yes sir!" Terry had responded with the other Captains. Talking about being polite while being screamed at, Terry couldn't help but smile.

Terry scanned the streets seeing his men and women smiling as they walked the streets. Some were speaking to people in stores or on the sidewalks. He sighed thinking he hoped all his people were polite.

Terry dropped his smile seeing a large Law Enforcement officer walking toward him. He watched the man as he stopped in front of him. The man was not smiling.

"Well I'm glad to see the military is here to save us." The Commander said sarcastically. Terry looked at him without speaking. The Commander looked around then said, looking at Terry. "If you need any assistance you be sure to call. I have men that can handle any situation. "I'm not sure why you are here?"

Terry did not speak as he looked at the big man. The Commander continued to look at Terry. Finally Terry in a low voice said, "thank you Commander."

Commander Miller did not speak. He stood quietly next to Terry watching the street. "Why are you here Captain?"

"Captain First Class. That's my title. I have orders to be here to make sure the peace is kept."

"I can do that myself." The Commander said snarling.

"You didn't handle the riot very well. Allowing civilians to be beaten up. Were you afraid to get involved, Commander?"

Commander Miller's face was deep blue. He turned to look at Terry. "It was under control." He growled.

"Yeah, we all saw on the broadcast how it was under control. So to be clear my orders are to make sure you and your goons who are left on the force are kept under control."

"How do you plan on doing that? I doubt you could handle my officers, or me."

"That won't be a problem. I'll give you a beating. It will be a professional beating." Terry said, staring directly at Miller."

"Just what is a professional beating?" Commander Miller asked, laughing.

"I won't enjoy it. Just a good professional beat down."

Commander Miller looked at Terry then turned and walked away.

Journalists were on the streets interviewing the Military men and women. Each of them had been briefed, so their answers were polite. The Journalist reported on all the conspiracies that were posted and were able to find a few of the radicals who insisted the Military were poised to take over the planet. Most people laughed at the crazies.

In the early afternoon all journalists gathered in front of the hospital. They watched as Shirley Franklin walked down the steps. She stopped in front of the large crowd. "My husband is recovering from his injuries. It will be a slow recovery. I have been researching the mob that gathered at the courthouse. It is clear outside thugs were brought in to stir up the crowd." Her eyes narrowed. "It took me only a few minutes to identify the outside agitators. None of you professional journalists have even looked for the reason there was a violent riot. I have not heard much from any of you questioning Premier Reverend Juddings who encouraged the mob to fight! Just what is your job? Are you and your networks afraid to confront Reverend Juddings, or the Master Chief? All you want is sensational reporting. You think the people of this planet are stupid. Go do your jobs and try some investigative reporting. Report the facts!"

Shirley turned walking away as tears fell from her eyes. The Journalist followed her asking questions. Two military men walking beside her pushed the yelling journalists back.

That evening on the monitors as people watched the broadcast journalist reported how outside agitators had been placed within the protestors. Some of the protestors left when the violence started. Many became involved in fighting law enforcement. When asked what Law Enforcement was doing about the riot. Master Chief Jackson said he was looking into the rumor of outside agitators, but he was not able to prove this rumor. When asked how many people had been arrested who were involved in the riot. Jackson smiled saying "riot is a strong word. It was a disturbance."

He did not comment on the terminated officers or those who had resigned. The broadcast was brutal as journalists recounted many of the other scandals Master Chief Jackson had been involved with in the past.

Reverend Juddings could not be reached for comment concerning his call to action to defend the church. Journalists reported on the fact that many people were leaving the Shelet church.

# Chapter XVIII

JOURNALISTS GATHERED in front of the Shelet church. The large stone church was built on a hill. Beautiful stained glass windows, with intricate carved doors enhanced the church entry. Massive circular spires that reached for the heavens on each side of the doors were impressive.

The journalists waited anxiously as a press conference had been called for that afternoon.

Premier Reverend Juddings opened the large carved door and walked down the beautiful delicate steps to where the journalists were waiting. They were all surprised to see him not wearing a robe or a hat. He was dressed in regular clothes like any other person. He looked tired and worn out.

Reverend Juddings held up his hand speaking softly "Please I ask there be no questions until I finish." He looked at the many journalists that had gathered. Most had cameras. He smiled slightly. "I am confused. I have been in prayer to our Lord. Recent events that have occurred, I find troubling. I am saddened by what I saw on the broadcast, people being beaten. Our Law Enforcement officers not responding to give assistance. When those brave officers who did respond to help those who were attacked by a mob were fired, that is troubling. I do not understand how Master Chief Jackson who has been a loyal member of this church could allow this to happen. I believe the carousel project is an abomination. It is wrong, and blasphemous. However, to resort to violence is not the answer. My words did not incite a violent mob who attacked the Franklins and injured Law Enforcement officers. My words were perfect, and were in line with the sacred word. I do not understand why Chief Jackson would terminate those Officers who defended the Franklins. That is not with our teaching of Shelet doctrine. Now I am hearing of outside agitators, thugs who were brought in to cause a problem. I pray Law Enforcement had nothing to do with them. I am shocked, I would never condone such actions. I believe we should all pray and seek the Lord's guidance."

Emerial turned and walked up the steps as journalists followed him asking questions. He opened the doors and walked in. Men stood in the doorway not allowing Journalists inside.

Shirley sat in Eric's hospital room watching the broadcast. "How humble you are now Reverend." she said frowning

THE FOLLOWING MORNING Journalists rushed to the headquarters of the Law Enforcement offices. They stood on the sidewalk anxiously waiting for Master Chief Jackson to appear. His office had called a press conference. When the doors opened Master Chief Jackson walked out and down the steps. He was wearing his formal dress uniform. Journalists immediately began yelling questions. He stood quietly surveying the mob of yelling journalists.

William Jackson raised his hand, "quiet, I need all of you to quiet down so I can speak."

The journalists grew silent. William held up a piece of paper. "I am here today to announce my resignation effective immediately."

Journalists immediately began yelling and asking questions. William stood quiet. He held up his hand. "Quiet!" He yelled. "You're all Idiots who prove how unprofessional you truly are!" The journalists mumbled to each other then became silent. "I have chosen to resign because it is time. I have served this City for many solar cycles. I have always done what I thought was best for this city. Sometimes I have erred in my judgment, but I did what I thought was best for the city. I am past my time to retire. I hate all of you journalists because you are so stupid. You do not report news, but make up stories as you and your network see fit. I hope each of you die a terrible senseless death." He gave them all an obscene gesture then walked down the sidewalk toward the capitol across the street.

Journalists were enraged. They followed him asking questions which he ignored. When they tried to get in front of him he pushed them out of the way. He refused to answer questions as they all yelled at him.

William Jackson walked across the street to the capitol building. He walked through the doors and to the escalator where he rode it to the top floor. Stepping off the escalator he walked to a door and walked into a large office. He saw standing in the office was the city's Mayor Pam Humphries. William handed her the paper.

"My resignation, Mayor Humphries. I know you have been waiting for this day for many cycles. I don't like you and never have. I would ask you to have a pleasant day, but really I hope you fall off the escalator, break your neck, and die with your skirt above your head."

William walked out of the office as journalists yelled at him. Exiting the building he stepped into a waiting car. He gave the journalists a final obscene gesture and cursed them all as the car left quickly. He and his wife boarded a shuttle and left the planet.

MAYOR PAM HUMPHRIES appointed David Parker as Master Chief of Law Enforcement. David had served as a Deputy for many lunar cycles. He immediately rehired all terminated officers, giving them each a citation for valor. All other officers were reinstated with a raise. Those who did not assist in the riot were demoted. Commander

Miller was demoted to the property room. David thanked the Military for their assistance and advised they could stand down. The Military were relieved of duty and returned to their regular posts. No charges were brought against Jackson since nothing could be proven.

# Chapter XIX

SHIRLEY WALKED INTO Eric's room seeing him awake. She walked to his bed kissing him on the forehead. "How are you feeling Eric?"

"Great, I may jump out of bed and go for a long walk with the most beautiful woman on this planet."

"I don't think so, honey. The Doctor says you will come home in a few days, but you will need to rest."

Shirley sat down in a soft chair. "I have some news. Master Chief David Parker is working on bringing those hooligans to justice. He is using artificial intelligence with a face recognition program to apprehend the bad guys. It's funny he has made a lot of arrests when Jackson couldn't find any of the suspects. I've been told I can not serve as a judge on any of the cases of the riot."

"Imagine that," Eric said, smiling. "I have no doubt you would be fair."

Shirley smiled "Oh, by the way did you catch the broadcast of the Jackson press conference?"

Eric laughed then held his side as it throbbed in pain. "Yes," he gasped. "I thought it was befitting of a jerk like him. What an idiot."

Shirley smiled. "I have a friend who works for Mayor Humphries. She was hopping mad, but also glad to get Jackson's resignation. She has had him under investigation for many lunar cycles. Anyway he is gone and the planet is better for it."

"Did you see the Reverend's press conference?" Eric asked.

"Yes he is trying to distance himself from his behavior. He needs to understand words are important. He all but called for a riot. His mob of thugs gave him what he wanted. Now he is trying to talk his way out of it." Shirley sat up. "You know Law Enforcement has caught many involved in the riot at the shuttle port trying to leave the planet. They have all said they were paid to come to Praque to cause as many problems as they could. They even broke into the University and tore up a lot of offices. Your office was one of them. The money to pay the thugs has been traced to an account on Halifax, but no one has been able to find who opened the account or who is responsible for putting in the money. Halifax has a pretty liberal banking system."

Eric lay quiet, "Hal came by and said my office was tore up pretty bad. They were not able to get in since Law Enforcement was investigating."

Later that afternoon Doctor Sanford and his wife Betsy walked into the room. Shirley stood up and hugged them both. "It is good to see you both." She said smiling.

"We wanted to check on Eric to make sure he and you are doing alright." Betsy said concerned.

"Both of us are doing well." Shirley said, " Eric will come home in a few days."

"Good,"Roger said smiling. He needs to be back at work teaching, and researching, I don't pay him to lay around you know."

"Oh, now Roger, don't be so grouchy. Eric needs his rest." Betsy said smiling. She took Shirley's hand "by the way Judge Franklin have you had a chance to look into this citation that was wrongfully and illegally given?"

"Betsy, Stop it. Shirley has been through a lot and I'm sure has not had time to look into this petty matter. You need to just pay the fine."

"He's being grumpy again." Betsy said laughing.

Shirley smiled, "It's been taken care of Betsy."

Betsy smiled.

Roger walked up to Eric's bed. "I do have some bad news. Law Enforcement had me come to your office. The carousel was destroyed by the mob who broke into your office. I'm so sorry Eric."

Eric lay quietly for a while then said. "Well Doctor Sanford, I don't think so. After the hearing at the capitol, and the protesters, I was concerned about the carousel. I took one of the other older carousel's and put in an artificial intelligence virtual reality program that copied the original one. I hid the original carousel in a safe place."

Roger smiled, "I am relieved to hear that. I thought we had lost the carousel. Good thinking on your part Eric. Where is the carousel hidden?"

"In the library." Eric said smiling.

Roger was stunned. "The library? How is that safe?"

"When was the last time you were in the library?"

"Well it has been a while I suppose."

Eric's smile grew wider, "you can't even remember the last time you were in the library. Noone goes to the library anymore. It's a museum. Trust me it's safe."

Roger laughed. "I believe you are correct Doctor Franklin. The library is the perfect place to hide the carousel. We don't even have a librarian anymore. It is a museum."

Betsy's eyes narrowed, "say Roger wasn't the last Librarian Mrs. Collins? Wasn't she your Primary teacher in your first year?"

"Yes I suppose she was. I had forgotten about that. After she retired we used artificial intelligence to assist students."

Betsy laughed. "You were afraid of old Roxie! The head of the University didn't go into the library because you were afraid of your old teacher!"

"That is not true." Roger insisted. You need to show more respect for the Elders." Roger smiled. "She was a little scary. She would remind me of not being a good student. I swear she never aged. She looked the same as when I was in Primary School. She always wore her hair in a bun."

Betsy laughed. "She called you naughty Roger."

"You are confused again." he took Betsy's hand "We need to go." he looked at Eric. "I'll check on the carousel."

That evening as Eric had finished his supper Anne Hamilon walked into his room. Shirley stood up walking to her, placing her small hand on Anne's cheek. "It is so good to see you, Elder Hamilton."

Anne smiled, "Oh, Mrs. Franklin how are you? I have been so concerned after seeing the broadcast."

"I and Eric are both fine. Eric is healing and should be home in a few days."

Anne walked to Eric holding his hand as tears fell from her eyes. "You were so brave, Doctor Franklin, You protected your wife from that terrible mob. I was so ashamed seeing Law Enforcement standing and watching you take that beating. I was glad to see some of the officers had moral courage."

"Thank you Elder Hamilton, you honor me." Eric said quietly

Anne sat down in a chair. "I won't stay long. I did speak to Betsy who said you were feeling better. I just wanted to come by and see you."

"We are both glad you did Elder Hamilton." Shirley said softly.

"Have you been able to determine anything about the carousel? I have been watching it on my monitor. It is so intriguing watching the people inside. They do not seem much different than we are."

"I believe they are not much different. It appears human nature whether ours or theirs is actually very similar."

"I did speak to Reverend Wallace, he is Omniprest, He believes this may be the work of the Lord. He may well have created the tiny beings. What do you think, Doctor Franklin?" Anne asked as she leaned back in her chair watching Eric.

"I believe that is possible. I can not prove scientifically how the small people inside the carousel were created. I suppose divine intervention is possible."

Anne smiled as she stood up slowly. "I believe our Lord may have a sense of irony." She hugged Shirley then left the room.

# Chapter XX

OFFICER BILL MYERS walked into the Secondary School Science room of second year students. The instructor Rick Kibbe stopped talking, seeing the officer in uniform.

"I need to speak with Robert Burks." He announced, raising his voice.

A tall young man stared at the officer, "I'm Robert Burks."

Officer Myers walked directly to the young man grasping his arm helping him to stand up. He walked the young man to the back of the room and out of the door.

Rick followed him out of the classroom, he was obviously concerned. "Officer, what is the meaning of this? Robert is a good student. He is from a good family. I don't understand."

Officer Myers continued to walk down the wide hallway without speaking.

"I didn't do anything! There must be a mistake! You have made a big mistake, officer. My Father is an important man!" Robert was scared and in a panic.

At the end of the hallway the head chancellor stood staring at the three men. As they approached, he said, "Mr. Kibbe, I need to speak to you."

Rick Kibbe stopped as the head chancellor took his arm. He watched Officer Myers and Robert walk out of the school.

Officer Myers stopped his vehicle in front of Law Enforcement Headquarters. He escorted Robert holding his arm into the building. An older man stood up, his face blue with anger. "What is the meaning of this! You can't arrest my son! I demand to know what is happening?" Todd Burks yelled.

Officer Myers continued to walk, stopping at a door. He opened it stepping inside with Robert. Todd and Dale Hastings, who was an attorney, followed him inside. Doctor Eric Franklin and David Parker stopped talking looking at the men. Officer Myers stepped back, closing the door standing against the wall.

"I demand to know what is going on! My son, arrested! I will have all of you in court!" Todd screamed.

"Calm down Todd," Dale said looking at Todd. he turned to David, "what is going on here? Why was Robert arrested."

David stood up, his face showed no emotion. He looked at Robert pointing to a chair. "Sit down."

"What is going on! Why are you treating my son like a criminal! Todd screamed.

David leaned forward. "If you raise your voice again, I will have officer Myers remove you." His stare was unblinking as he looked at Todd. David turned to Dale.

"You and Mr. Burks will sit down. I will not have a disturbance or trouble from either of you. Do you understand?"

Dale nodded, taking Todd's arm. "You need to calm down. Let's find out what is going on."

Dale sat next to Robert as Todd sat down glaring at David.

David stared at Robert. "You are Robert Burks?"

"Yes." he replied quietly.

"You attend Phram secondary school in the north west quadrant?"

"Yes."

"You hacked into the Universities computers and changed the parameters of the recent carousel project that was on display." David stated, looking directly at Robert.

"Don't answer that." Dale said quickly.

The room fell silent. David said "You can leave if you choose. This is just a preliminary investigation. Robert is not under arrest." David leaned back saying "Doctor Franklin."

Eric sat forward, his face was blue with anger. "The carousel parameters have been changed. I traced the computer back to your personal computer. You instructed the computer to create an alien craft. It crashed onto the planet called Earth. The inhabitants were able to reverse engineer the craft and now have advanced tremendously in their technology. There have also been other crafts the computer has created because it was not told to stop. You interfered with the natural development of an emerging species." Eric sat back, he was obviously upset.

No one spoke. David leaned forward. "You can speak to me, or not. I will file charges and you will finish your studies behind bars in a juvenile facility. When you graduate you will be sent to prison."

"You can't do that!" Todd yelled.

David pointed to Todd, "remove this gentleman officer Myers.

Todd was dragged out of the room. "You can leave now if you want. It is obvious you do not want to talk." David said, looking directly at Dale.

Dale stood up, taking Robert's arm. "We're leaving. Robert."

When Robert and Dale had left Eric started to stand up. "No, have a seat Doctor Franklin. They'll be back."

Eric looked at David who sat back in his chair. "You want some tea, Doctor Franklin?"

"Sure,"

David stood up walking around the table and out of the door. Eric watched him leave. He knew he had a lot of work to do at the

University. He wanted to return to work, and didn't see how sitting in the small conference room would accomplish anything. The other men had left

When Eric had been released from the hospital he had intended on going back to work. Shirley insisted he stay home and recover. He had been away from the carousel for three lunar cycles.

When he returned to the University he had gone to his office. Doctor Sanford had removed the old carousel from the library and placed it in his office. He had the University maintenance department install a reinforced door on his office suite entrance, as well as on his office.

He was shocked looking through the viewer how the small inhabitants had advanced so quickly in technology. They had communication satellites orbiting their planet. They had left their planet visiting their moon. Space probes had been sent to the fourth planet. A sophisticated space lab orbited their planet. A computer system with superior capabilities was assisting the people to advance quickly.

He had found where Robert had hacked into the computer creating a flying saucer that he was using as a probe for the planet. The flying saucer had made designs in crops planted by the small humanoid people. Eric was furious seeing how the flying saucer was used to conduct experiments on the planet and the inhabitants. When it crashed the people were able to advance their technology greatly. The computer continued to create flying crafts which flew around the Earth, many of them crashing in different areas of the planet. He had shut down the illegal experiment immediately. Eric was able to trace the hacker to Robert's home computer. He notified Law Enforcement immediately. He was surprised, but pleased The Master Chief Law Enforcement officer had chosen to be involved.

David walked in carrying two cups. He sat one down in front of Eric. He smiled as he sat down. "Sorry for taking so long. I had to call Emier Norton. It seems Todd Burks is an influential man, and the Emier wanted a briefing. He is talking to Representatives letting them know this should not be a political matter. Law Enforcement needs to handle it."

Eric stared into his coffee cup then looked at David. "Why would it be political? This is a matter for Law Enforcement."

David smiled as he sipped his tea. He sat the cup down. "Todd Burks is a powerful man with a lot of wealth. His son is in trouble facing prison time. It will no doubt be political."

"You may have been harsh in telling the young man he was going to prison." Eric said, picking up his cup.

David smiled, "well you have to start with an extreme sometimes to get people's attention. We can now negotiate."

# Chapter XXI

After an hour Officer Myers stepped into the room. "They want to talk, Chief." He smiled and stepped back leaning against the back wall.

Robert, Todd, and Dale walked into the room. Todd sat down leaning back staring at David. Dale cleared his throat. "Chief, Doctor Franklin, my client may have made a mistake, being a curious young man. He is extremely bright and is currently at the top of his class. I believe we can come to an agreement prior to charges being filed."

David sat quietly looking at Dale. He looked at Robert without speaking. The room was quiet as the tension grew. David continued to stare at Robert without speaking. Finally Todd said in a controlled voice. "I do have friends in high places that could get involved. It could be, say, unpleasant for you Chief."

David looked at Todd then looked back at Robert. He stood up looking at Eric.

"We're through here Doctor Franklin."

Eric stood up and walked out of the room with David.

Dale rubbed his face with his hands. "I asked you not to speak, Todd. Let me do all the talking. Now you have blown up any deal that we might have reached."

"I'm not going to let that man put my son in prison, Dale!" Todd yelled as he leaned forward.

"You want this to get ugly and public. I assure you it will." Dale stood up, "you need to find another attorney. I'm out." Dale walked out of the room leaving Todd and Robert sitting alone. Todd followed Dale begging him not to quit, he needed him.

Emier Ron Norton looked up from his paperwork seeing several Representatives, with Todd Burks walk into his office. He did not smile. The men sat down in front of the desk. Ron said, "I know why you are here. I will tell you now, I will not be getting involved in a matter that is for Law Enforcement. If you choose to allow this situation to become political you will not have my support."

"Why not!" Todd yelled. "This is ridiculous, my son is not a criminal! He's not going to Prison, for an indiscretion!"

"Your son Illegally broke into a secure computer system at the University and tampered with an ongoing project. It is a matter for the judicial system." he leaned back looking at the men. "If you want to get involved I will convene a hearing to investigate this matter. Many people on this planet and off planet are extremely upset the carousel project has not been available for them to watch. I have spoken with Head Chancellor Sanford asking him to resume the project." He leaned forward. "I believe it would be appropriate to open an investigation. I will send an official request to Representative Gymini's office so a proper hearing may be conducted."

Jordan felt uncomfortable as he looked at Emier Norton. "Ron, I don't believe a hearing would be not appropriate at this time. The courts have not completed their investigation, a decision has not been determined yet."

"You have held hearings in the past prior to a court decision. I can't think of a better opportunity than now. The public is angry the carousel project has not been available to watch. Now that a breach has occurred and the inhabitants are now farther along with technology. I'm sure they will want to get to the truth. You want the truth, don't you, Representative Gymini?"

"Hold it right there!" Todd was on his feet. "You're wanting to set my son up!

I won't hear of it!" Todd screamed.

"Don't raise your voice to me in my office. You were invited, so show some courtesy to this office." Ron stood up. "You want me to call Master Chief Parker and stop this investigation? I doubt he would listen. His ethics would not allow him to be pressured to stop a legal investigation, and my morals will not allow me to stoop to such dirty politics. I assure you this is a serious matter. It is a matter for Law Enforcement. Now all of you are excused."

The men left the office.

Representative Jordan Gymini later received an official request to open an investigative hearing into the carousel being broken into by a computer hacker. He sat quietly knowing he had a problem. If he opened the investigation with his hearing, it would mean Robert would be required to testify. If he did not open a hearing on the matter, it would make him look petty and show his biasness. He would wait and hope this would blow over.

Journalists were in a frenzy when the carousel was placed back on line. The explanation that an individual had broken into the system and changed the parameters was a shock to everyone. The Burks family were swarmed by journalists. Journalists were brutal to the Burks family.

The computer system was made safe with a stronger firewall, and there were no worries of it being tampered with by outside forces. When the journalists asked Doctor Franklin, and Doctor Sanford for an update they received the same answer, "the investigation was still ongoing."

Master Chief Parker ignored the Journalists, refusing to speak to them.

Todd Burks soon discovered his wealth and prestige could not gain him any favors. He was an elitist whose wealth had gained him many favors with the government. There was a backlash from the public for being an elite member of society.

The Government Representatives, who all had a political nature, realized their constituents were angry over the carousel. It would not be politically correct to get involved on the wrong side. Most sided with the public outraged at the hacking into a University computer. Others remained quiet.

Representative Gymini explained to journalists, the matter was a Law Enforcement concern and he had complete confidence in Master Chief Parker to be fair. He insisted the Courts should handle the matter seeing no need to open an investigation. He told the eager journalists he would wait and see, and if needed he could open an investigation with a formal hearing later.

Robert Burks who was an arrogant individual because of his Father's money, and the fact he was very intelligent was scared. He had thought it was funny to break into the computer system and run his own experiments on the inhabitants of Earth. He laughed at the paranoid people and watched as each government denied the existence of Unidentified Flying Objects. Now he was scared of going to prison.

Dale Hastings was able to work out a deal with the courts where Robert was placed on House Arrest. He would be able to finish his schooling at home. The next two years he could attend school but was restricted in his movements. He was to be at home when not in school. A large fine was imposed, and he was required to work at a shelter for those individuals who were poor, as well as having issues with mental health. He hated it, but was afraid to not complete his court required mandate.

Eric installed a backup generator that would run if for some reason the original generator stopped working. The carousel would continue to run as the planets continued to move in their orbits around the sun. The people of Praque and other planets watched in fascination as the small inhabitants went on with their daily lives. Schools would use the carousel as an example for students to learn how societies evolved. Scientists would study every aspect of the project attempting to explain how it was possible for life to be created. They never did find an answer. The Religious community would argue the facts according to their interpretation of the sacred word, but most people simply believed it was an act of God. A miracle that could not be explained.

# Chapter XXII

THE PEOPLE ON THE PLANET, Halifax had lived under the burden of a rigid religious order for many solar cycles. Their freedom of worshiping their religion they had been raised to believe for eons had been taken from them. There was only one religion, they had to adhere to that religion or face prosecution for worshiping as their ancestors had for many generations. Many were fined for not attending services and paying tithes.

Most of the inhabitants of Halifax were colonists who had moved to the planet when it was terraformed many solar cycles ago. The original native people of Halifax were in the minority and seen as odd, with strange customs. The native people were a light color reddish brown, with light hair. They were usually smaller in stature than the colonists.

They had strange rituals where once a year they would go into the wilderness and practice their strange religion. Law enforcement would ignore them and not bother to challenge them. It was technically against the law, but the indigenous people did not present any danger to the community so their practice was ignored. Most people accepted the native Halifax people and their odd ways. If there was an arrest of them practicing their religion. Many on the planet would protest such treatment. So it was easier to look the other way.

When the broadcast of the carousel project was received on Halifax. The native people were fascinated with the strange people inside the carousel. They were transfixed with the different cultures and studied them closely.

They studied how Native Americans on the American continent and how they were treated poorly by colonists from the European continent caught their attention. They saw how the people called Aborigines of the continent Australia were treated and their homeland was taken and were marginalized in their own country. The Irish, treated poorly by English, Roman conquest and how people were brutalized, and many other cultures that were invaded and colonized.

When the indigenous people of Halifax studied the religious texts they were most intrigued with the fact there were many different religions. They were fascinated with the religion Christianity. Specifically Jesus of Nazarath. They were intrigued with how the Jewish religion could split off to become Islam, Christian, then Catholic and Protestant.

The words of Jesus touched them and all began to believe this man called Rabi, and some called Messiah, who was crucified for speaking the truth, would understand their cause. They began to question why they were still forced to have one religion, when in the carousel on the planet Earth there was freedom of religion throughout most of civilization.

Halifax indigenous people began to gather and ask, why not have freedom from religion. There should be freedom of religion where a person could worship as they chose, not as they were forced. The gatherings became larger and many joined the conversation. Soon there were many people who began to question why the Government and Religious sector were so closely tied. They were expected to give a tithe of their earnings which if they did not the Government would impose a penalty on them. The freedom from religion began to grow.

The large crowds would become loud and often with inspiring speakers it soon was apparent that trouble could soon become violent. The gathering crowds were seen on other planets and soon many of the people across the galaxy began to spread the message that there should be freedom of religion. Individuals should have the right to choose to worship as they want without interference from the Government.

The Government of Praque soon had to deal with the issue of Religion. Since there had been so many issues lately with Religion and the controversy with the Shelet beliefs, people were questioning why the Government was involved in Religious services.

Many Government Representatives began to argue there could be no change to the system that had been established and if there was a change then it could be seen as an insult to God. The Government was to protect religion. The religious leaders would advise and help lead the nation's leaders. Others disagreed saying God was not concerned with the Government, but with the souls of men. Many people pointed out it was not religion, but the Shelet view of how things in the government should occur.

Emier Norton made it clear he believed Government and Religion should be separate. He asked Representatives to send him a bill that would separate the Government completely from Religious services. He made it clear the laws that forbid worshiping religion other than that approved or questioning religion should be overturned.

Premier Revend Juddings was vehemently against this and made it clear Emier Norton had lost his soul. He gave long sermons about how there was only one God and one Religion. Those who opposed him would perish. He was God's ambassador and he spoke for the Lord. To question him was to question the Lord.

The Omnipresent religious leaders who were usually quiet on the issue of religion, now spoke out loudly. They insisted religious beliefs should be a choice. Noone should be forced to believe. They backed Emier Norton.

Only a few people who were elitist listened to Reverend Juddings. They however were now in the minority. He had lost credibility with most people. He was seen as an elitist who had lived very well as other people often struggled to survive. The people of Praque had grown tired of the unfair taxes and laws that benefited the wealthy elite. Instead of being separated by beliefs and politics, people sat their differences aside and came together to protest. The people stood as one.

Those politicians who were savvy enough to see the change in beliefs made it clear they were with the common people. A law of freedom of Religion was soon passed allowing individuals freedom to worship as they chose. Government would no longer impose penalties that burden those who did not comply.

The old religion on Halifax came out from underground and practiced in the open. Their religion of worshiping a God that had created the universe and had given a soul to all living things was no longer prohibited. The native people knew when they died all would go to a place that was similar as it had been on Halifax. Their fight had not only won the people of Halifax their freedom to worship as they chose, but allowed those across the galaxy to also be free to worship, or not.

Shirley Franklin sitting with Eric watching the broadcast cried as she saw an injustice undone. "Praise the Lord," she whispered.

Shirley wiped her eyes, "do you think we are an experiment from a higher intelligence. Perhaps a student has created a carousel where we are living in an existence, where we are a microcosm being watched by someone else?"

Eirc smiled broadly. "I have no doubt we were created by a higher power."

THE SMALL PEOPLE OF the Earth inside the old carousel were not aware of the outside world, believing they were the only people created. How they were created would be an argument that was never solved.

They would continue to believe no other planets were inhabited. And, in a way they were correct, none of the other planets in their galaxy were inhabited. Many of the Earth people would wonder as they stared at the stars if there was life somewhere in another galaxy.

The people of Earth being oblivious to the greater outside world that watched their planet, continued to live their lives as they believed was best. They would never know how their culture had changed the lives of many people across a vast galaxy.

Perhaps the Lord does have a sense of irony.

the end

# Don't miss out!

Visit the website below and you can sign up to receive emails whenever RB Parkline publishes a new book. There's no charge and no obligation.

https://books2read.com/r/B-A-PNYC-UPYWC

**BOOKS 2 READ**

Connecting independent readers to independent writers.